Kathleen O'Meara

Narka

Vol. II

Kathleen O'Meara

Narka
Vol. II

ISBN/EAN: 9783337047740

Printed in Europe, USA, Canada, Australia, Japan

Cover: Foto ©Andreas Hilbeck / pixelio.de

More available books at **www.hansebooks.com**

N A R K A.

A Novel.

BY

KATHLEEN O'MEARA,

AUTHOR OF ' FREDERIC OZANAM,' ' IZA'S STORY,' ' MADAME MOHL, HER SALON
AND HER FRIENDS,' ' THE OLD HOUSE IN PICARDY,' ETC., ETC.

IN TWO VOLUMES.
VOL. II.

LONDON:
RICHARD BENTLEY AND SON,
Publishers in Ordinary to Her Majesty the Queen.
1888.

CONTENTS OF VOL. II.

CHAPTER   PAGE

I. THIS IS MY GOOD FRIEND, DR. SCHENK - 1

II. THE IMPRESARIO - 16

III. DR. SCHENK IN ATTENDANCE ON NARKA - 29

IV. NARKA AT LA VILLETTE - 37

V. NARKA EXPOUNDS THE GOSPEL OF THIS WORLD - 50

VI. THE DOWNWARD STEP - 59

VII. THE MEETING IN THE QUARTIER LATIN - 67

VIII. GOLD IN THE DROSS - 89

IX. SIBYL MAKES ACQUAINTANCE WITH LA VILLETTE - 96

X. RUMBLINGS OF THE STORM - 117

XI. LA VILLETTE IN ARMS - 127

XII. NARKA'S LULLABY - 141

XIII. MARGUERITE DISOBEYS THE LAW - 149

XIV. NARKA SINGS FOR JOY - 161

CHAPTER   PAGE

XV. 'IN THE NAME OF THE EMPEROR!' - - 173

XVI. THE PRIDE OF THE ZOROKOFFS - - 185

XVII. IN THE VISION OF THE NIGHT - - 208

XVIII. PENDING THE TRIAL - - - - 226

XIX. IN COURT - - - - - 232

XX. LARCHOFF'S MURDERER - - - 257

XXI. 'I HAVE NEVER LOVED ANY WOMAN AS I LOVED

YOU' - - - - - - 269

XXII. RENUNCIATION - - - - 287

XXIII. LA SCALA - - - - - 306

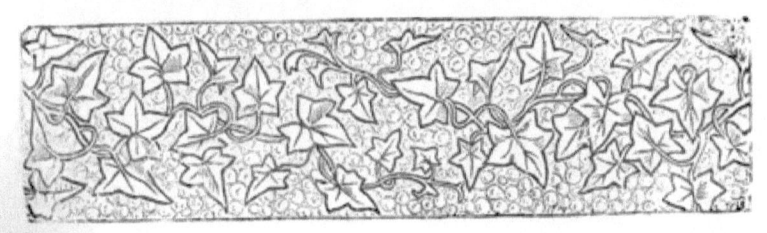

NARKA.

—◦◦◦◦◦—

CHAPTER I.

'THIS IS MY GOOD FRIEND, DR. SCHENK.'

THE first thing Narka did on returning home was to give notice to the concierge that she meant to leave that day week. Then, obedient to Marguerite's wishes, she went to bed. The warmth and rest—or, as Narka preferred to believe, the virtue of Marguerite's cherishing sympathy which had passed into her remedies —had the effect of staving off the illness which had seemed to threaten her. She rose feeling little the worse physically for the violent emotions, the sleepless nights she had gone through, and the chill of yesterday.

In the afternoon, the concierge brought up a letter from the landlord in answer to the *congé*. It was a polite but distinct refusal to accept it. He regretted to remind his amiable tenant that she had signed an engagement to occupy, or pay for, the apartment up to April 15th. Narka uttered an exclamation of dismay; but, referring to the paper in question, she found that this was true : she was bound to her present expensive quarters for nearly three months longer. There was nothing to be done but trust to Providence to bring her safe out of this new difficulty, as out of so many others.

In its outward tenor her life remained, therefore, undisturbed, notwithstanding the violent change that had shaken it inwardly. Marguerite's plans, practical like herself, succeeded. Through a kind and wealthy South American lady, who was a benefactress to her poor, she procured at once several rich pupils for Narka, all foreigners, who came to her house twice a week for lessons and a general singing-class.

To Narka, Sibyl was affectionate as ever. She took a lively interest in the singing-class, and would come and sit and listen to the lesson, and bring out the superiority of the teacher's method by her clever criticisms, thus raising Narka's value in the eyes of the pupils and of their mothers, to whom the charming and *élégante* Comtesse de Beaucrillon was an oracle on art as well as fashion. The singing-lessons came in this way to be a pleasant social opportunity. Narka, moreover, might have led a gay life enough if she had been so inclined, for invitations poured in on her, but she refused them all.

' I know my value,' she said to Marguerite; these fine ladies would be glad enough to have me to help out their entertainments ; but if their sons or their brothers were the least bit civil to me, they would put me to the door. I shan't expose myself to that.

Let them stay in their place, and I will stay
in mine.'

She had not had a sign from Basil since
that terrible letter from the Prince, and there
was no one to whom she could even mention
his name, except Marguerite. Sibyl, as if
the subject were too intolerable, avoided it.
When she did speak of it, it was to pity
her father and herself, and to condemn Basil,
and wish the woman dead who had entrapped
him.

The only person who might have given
her any news of Basil was Ivan Gorff; but
he had left Paris as soon as he had conducted her there, and had never written
since, and she did not know his address.
There was, of late, something very mysterious about Ivan. Narka knew that he associated with the most advanced revolutionists,
yet he came and went perfectly free, while
Basil, for merely conniving at the movement
which Ivan was, she suspected, actively pre-
cipitating, had been seriously compromised,
only escaping imprisonment through a lucky

chance. Then Ivan was leading a strange
life for a man of thirty, in possession of a
fortune, which, since Sophie's death, must
be reckoned by millions.

His personal appearance suggested biting
economy, offensive slovenliness, or sordid
avarice, whereas in former days he had been
somewhat dandified in his dress, and generous
as a king. On the journey from Koenigs-
berg he had put up at a miserable inn at
Berlin, apologizing to Narka for taking her
there, but pleading as a reason that the
people were honest, and that he was in the
habit of staying there. What motive could
induce a man of his wealth to deprive himself not alone of luxuries, but of the comforts
that he had all his life been accustomed to ?

One afternoon, on coming home from a
lesson, Narka, who had been thinking a
great deal about Ivan, and wishing to hear
from him, found that in her absence he had
called and left word that he would call again
next morning. It was a bitter disappointment to have missed him ; he was sure to

have news of Basil; he had probably seen
him. She was too excited to sleep that night,
and counted the hours till morning. But
morning passed, and Ivan did not appear.
He had left no address, so she could not
write to him. The singing-class was at one
o'clock, and Narka's terror was that he would
call while it was going on, and that she
should miss him again. But the singing-
class came to an end, and there was still no
sign of him. Immediately after the lesson,
Sibyl came to take her for a drive. There
was no ostensible reason for refusing, so
Narka had to go.

It was the longest drive she ever took,
and Sibyl noticed that she was strangely
preoccupied. On returning home she found
a note from Ivan, saying he had been
hindered from coming by an accident, but
he hoped to see her in a few days. Narka
was too impatient to wait for his visit. The
note contained his address, so early the next
morning she set out to see him.

The Rue B——, where he was staying,

was a narrow sort of lane-way behind the Pantheon ; the house a shabby-looking *maison meublée.*

'Yes, monsieur is at home,' the concierge said, giving her the number of the room on the fifth story.

Narka did not stop to think of the proprieties. She mounted the dark stairs, steep and narrow as a ladder, and knocked at No. 96.

'Come in,' said a voice.

She opened the door. It was a small attic room, full of tobacco smoke, with the roof slanting on one side ; no fire, no carpet. Ivan was sitting in a high-backed armchair, buttoned to his chin in a huge furred coat, a pipe in his mouth, his head swathed to an enormous size in a woollen scarf. He looked like some grotesque caricature of a man.

'Narka Larik!' he said, removing his pipe, and his blue eyes widened and sparkled with that inarticulate laughter which gave to his countenance its peculiar expression of childlike candour and merriment.

'I thought something must have happened, as you did not keep your appointment.' Narka replied. 'You have met with an accident?'

'No; only a fierce fit of pain that seized me like a tiger. It knocked me over in an hour. I was half mad. But it is gone now. Schenk pricked me with morphine, and killed the pain.'

'Schenk?' said Narka interrogatively.

'He is a doctor; a very clever fellow, and a friend of mine. Sit down, won't you?'

He pushed toward her the armchair he had been occupying—the only one in the room.

What could have reduced Ivan Gorff to these extremities?

'When did you arrive in Paris?' Narka asked.

'The day before yesterday. I have come straight from St. Petersburg without drawing bridle. I took cold on the journey. It was like travelling through Siberia.'

Narka bethought herself that if he had

travelled first-class he would not have had
to complain of the cold.

' You saw Basil ?' she said.

' Yes.   He is well, but as savage as a
bear.   He and the Prince quarrel all day.
Basil has got himself into a fine dilemma.
He ought to have kept his affairs to himself,
at least for a while longer.'

' It was not he who told the Prince of our
engagement.   Some one whom he had trusted
with the secret betrayed him.'

' He ought not to have trusted anybody
with it.   He ought never to have put a line
on paper about it.   I warned him many a
time to be cautious, that the police had their
eyes and ears everywhere ; but it was no
use.   What did you do with those papers of
his ?'

' I have them safe with me.'

' That is foolish.   You ought to burn
them.   They may get you into trouble
again.'

' How could they ?   What do the police
know about me here ?'

Ivan's round eyes widened and twinkled until it seemed as if they were going to explode with laughter.

'You fancy the police don't know just as much about you here as if you were in St. Petersburg? You are very naïve, Narka Larik.'

'Am I? Well, you have something more interesting to say than that, have you not? Tell me about the Prince and Basil. The Prince wrote to Sibyl that if Basil did not surrender within three months he would have him sent to Kronstadt, and forbidden to leave the town until he came to his senses. Do you think he is capable of carrying out that threat?'

'He will try all soft means before he has recourse to the hard. He is trying to bribe Basil now with the promise of getting Father Christopher liberated and brought back to bless his marriage with Princess Krinsky.'

'Basil is not such a fool as to fall into that trap.'

Narka laughed.

'Humph!' Ivan moved his huge bundle
of a head slowly up and down. 'The Prince
is convinced that if he went to the Emperor
and told him the whole story, he would grant
Father Christopher's release at once. Marie
Krinsky is in love with Basil, and Prince
Krinsky is in high favour now. The
Empress, too, is greatly annoyed at Basil's
refusing to marry her pet maid-of-honour.
Basil knows all this; and then the thought of
Father Christopher's captivity haunts him
perpetually.'

Narka grew pale.

'The Emperor does not know about Basil's
supposed share in Larchoff's death?' she
asked.

'No; but Basil thinks he does. He never
heard, of course, of that tampering with his
letters.'

'Does the Prince know who it is that Basil
wants to marry?'

'He did not tell me if he did.'

'Basil would have told you?'

'Very likely, if he had had a chance; but

we were hardly five minutes alone. He wanted me to come next day and have a quiet talk; but I had not the time. I was obliged to leave the next morning.'

What could this business be that drove Ivan from city to city, compelling him to renounce the pleasure of a meeting with his best friend? Narka felt that she must know at all costs.

'Why cannot you trust me as Basil does?' she said, looking him straight in the eyes.

Ivan met her challenging glance with a beam of satisfaction.

'To trust our friends is sometimes the unkindest thing we can do. Basil proved that to you. But now that you are comparatively out of harm's way, I will tell you anything you care to know: I have thrown in my lot with those who want to do away with tyrants and set the nations free. This involves ways and means which those who don't want to risk their heads had better know nothing about. I don't care about

risking mine.   If it had gone while that
tigerish pain was clawing it yesterday, I
should have been glad enough.   But, on the
other hand, it would upset a lot of things if I
were to drop off now.   I am the telegraph
between all the centres.   There is not a plot
hatched anywhere but I am the first to hear
of it ; I carry messages that can't be written ;
I organize meetings ; I get the pamphlets
published ; I work the occult machinery of
the Socialist press, and direct its underground
operations.   All this gives me plenty to do.
It is not the work that brings pay and glory,
like the work of the hero in livery who
serves a tyrant, and calls it serving his
country ; but it is a hero's work, all the
same.   The man who undertakes it must
renounce everything and risk everything,
and live every day with death dogging him
like his shadow.'

Narka looked at Ivan with a new interest.
Assuredly no man ever presented a more un-
heroic appearance than he did, with his un-
gainly figure and his huge beturbaned head ;

nevertheless, she began to recognise in him a hero of some new and genuine, though perhaps dangerous, type.

'And is Basil involved in this work ?' she inquired.

'Yes; he has now thrown himself into it body and soul.'

'Ah !'

They were silent for a moment. Then Ivan said :

'Why should not you join us, Narka Larik ? You might help greatly, and without the same risk, here in France.'

'Show me how. Show me anything this head, or these hands, can do, and I will do it !' she answered impulsively.

Ivan held out his hand to her, and she laid hers in the broad palm that closed on it with a strong clasp. As they sat thus, hand in hand, the door opened, and a man came quickly in.

Narka recognised Dr. Schenk, and coloured violently.

'Oh, I am so glad you have come !' Ivan

said, slowly releasing her hand. 'This is
my good friend Dr. Schenk—Mademoiselle
Narka Larik, one of ours.'

Narka bowed, and stood up.

'Pray don't let me send you away, mademoiselle. I won't detain Gorff a minute,'
said Schenk.

'I was just going,' Narka replied, her
embarrassment relieved by his perfect ease
and respectful manner. 'I hope there is
nothing serious the matter with M. Gorff?'

'It is serious: a case of suicidal mania,'
observed the medical man. 'If he exercised
common humanity to himself he would be as
strong as a horse, but he maltreats himself as
if he were a dog.'

'I should not have thought you capable of
maltreating a dog,' Narka said, remembering
Marguerite's abuse of the vivisector.

She gave her hand again to Ivan, and
bowing coldly to Schenk, went out.

CHAPTER II.

THE IMPRESARIO.

ON reaching home Narka found a note from Sibyl, which a servant had just left. She opened the violet-scented missive, and read:

'MY DARLING,—I bring you a wonderful piece of good news!' (Narka stopped to take breath. Had Basil surrendered?) 'It has come so suddenly I can almost fancy it a fairy trick. Fortune is going to be kind to you, my Narka, and reward you after all you have suffered. Listen: I have just had a visit from Signor Zampa, who was director of the Italian Opera here last year, and is now managing La Scala, at Naples. He

gave me lessons when I came to Paris.
Well, dearest, he is in search of a soprano
voice to take the place of *prima donna* at La
Scala. An artist who heard you here on that
memorable night, carried the fame of your
voice and your genius to Naples, and Signor
Zampa has come on here to see if you would
suit him and accept his overtures. I gave
him your address, and with difficulty dis-
suaded him from rushing straight off to you,
there and then. I said he would not find
you till two o'clock, and I promised to send
word to you to expect his visit at two. I am
beside myself with delight ! Come to breakfast to-morrow morning, and meantime attune
your voice to its heavenliest key, and sing
the soul out of Zampa's breast, and millions
out of his pocket !

'Your own

'Sibyl.'

Narka dropped the letter with an inarticulate exclamation. She was bewildered. It
might, no doubt, be a most brilliant career

that was opened out unexpectedly to her, but at this first moment she could not realize anything but the shock of the proposal. To turn public singer, to go on the stage—she who was engaged to Prince Zorokoff? Was it possible to contemplate such a thing? And yet how was she to refuse it without incurring Sibyl's deep displeasure, rousing her suspicions, and in that case alienating her, perhaps irrevocably? And there was not even time to think it over.

It was just one o'clock, and Signor Zampa was likely to be punctual. She threw aside her bonnet, and went to the piano, and excitedly turned over the leaves of a music-book. She could not well refuse to sing for the impresario, if he asked her, and in the midst of her perplexity, the desire of the artist to win the approval of so great a critic asserted itself.

As the clock struck two, Signor Zampa rang at the door.

Narka, flushed with excitement, looked her best when he came in.

'You have heard from the Comtesse de Beaucrillon the object of my visit, mademoiselle ?' he said, conquered at once by her beauty.

'Yes. It has taken me by surprise. I never dreamed of going on the stage. I have not had the necessary training for it. I don't think I am at all fitted to be an opera singer.'

'Perhaps I am a better judge of that than you. Will you let me hear you sing ?'

She rose without any pretence of shyness, and went to the piano. Zampa pulled off his gloves.

'You will accompany me ?' she said.

'Certainly. What will you sing ?'

'Choose anything you like,' motioning indifferently to the books and songs that were scattered about.

'Let's try this,' he said, opening the partition of *Norma* at the 'Casta Diva.'

It happened to be a favourite piece of Narka's; she sang it well at all times, but, stimulated by his presence, she rendered it now with a perfection of art that must have delighted the *maestro*, even if her voice had not enchanted him by its rare qualities. When she ended, he burst out with a rapturous ' Brava!' and seizing her hand, kissed it with the demonstrative enthusiasm of his nation. He entreated her to sing several other pieces, each chosen with a view to bring out the various qualities of her voice. Narka, inspired by his admiration and discerning criticism, sang at her best, feeling that ecstasy in the expansion of her splendid powers which is by turns the triumph and the despair of every true artist. Every fibre in her was thrilling to the music of her voice. Something of the grand, untamed creature that was visible in her majestic lines and strong, supple limbs began to throb in her pulses and course in her blood; and when the Italian started up and described the brilliant future that was before her, she was more ready to respond to his offers than she could have believed possible an hour ago. As he stood there, with his fiery eloquence

and mercurial gesticulation, she could almost
fancy a wizard had sprung up on her path,
waving his wand, and bidding the mountains
roll down, and the desert blossom at her feet.

'You will be a star that will outshine every
star in the musical firmament of our age!' he
declared, executing a sort of war-dance on
the hearthrug in his excitement; 'all Europe
will ring with your fame ; crowned heads
will bow down before the royalty of your
genius!'

Narka listened, and felt something like
what the bird must feel when a kind hand is
about to open its cage and set it free to take
flight into its native element : she had been
beating the bars of her cage all her life, even
before she knew it.

Zampa saw that she was won, and he kept
throwing in the incense, till the fumes
enveloped her and went to her brain. It
was a delicious intoxication. But suddenly
the sweet smoke began to choke her : she
had forgotten Basil. What would he say?
How would this contemplated step affect

their common destiny ? Would the *prima donna* millionnaire be a more suitable wife for Prince Zorokoff than Narka Larik ?

' I am so taken by surprise,' she said, not attempting to disguise her emotion, ' that I cannot answer you to-day. I must have time to think over your proposal, and to consult .ny friends before I decide. I will write to you in a day or two.'

But the impresario went away confident and exulting. He had no doubt of having secured the prize.

When he was gone, Narka asked herself whether she was waking or dreaming. Had she done wisely in leaving him to believe she would entertain his offer ? As to consulting her friends, who had she to consult ? Sibyl would think her insane if she hesitated for a moment, and would never forgive her for rejecting an offer that she, Sibyl, so wholly approved of. There was Marguerite : Marguerite was sure to cry out in horror at the mere notion of the stage ; to her it would seem like walking into the lions' den. Still,

Narka must speak to some one, and there was only Marguerite, and Marguerite's sympathy was sure to be comforting, and it might possibly be illuminating.

Early next morning she set out to La Villette. To her great surprise, Marguerite, far from being horrified, met the idea complacently.

'I expected you would have shrieked at the bare notion of my risking my soul in such a wicked place as the theatre!' said Narka.

'Is it such a wicked place?' said Marguerite; 'I didn't know. A school friend of mine, a very pious girl, lost her fortune, and went on the stage, and sang for a year at the Opéra Comique, and she remained as pious as ever, and died like a little saint. But that was in Paris; perhaps at Naples it is worse.'

'I suspect it is the same everywhere, pretty much,' Narka replied. 'But I have no fear on that score,' she added, bridling inwardly; 'self-respect would protect me as well on the stage as walking about Paris alone. I was not thinking of any danger of that sort; it

does not exist for me.   I was thinking how
the thing will appear to Sibyl.'

'Sibyl ?   Why, Sibyl has invented it.'

'I mean about Basil.   Would it not be a
greater degradation for him to marry me if I
were a public singer ?'

'Ah !' Marguerite slipped her hands into
her wide sleeves, and put her head a little to
one side, and gave her whole mind to the
solution of this problem.   'Sibyl could tell
us,' she said, after a moment ; 'but we can't
ask Sibyl.'

'No, we can't ask Sibyl.'

They sat silent awhile.   Then Marguerite,
like a person who, having passed every
argument in review, arrives at a conclusion,
said :

'It always seems to me that the safest plan
is to take what Providence sends to us, and
trust the consequences to Him.   If you are
running no risk to your soul, I don't see why
you should not accept this offer.   Instead of
being an obstacle between you and Basil, it
may be the means of drawing you together.

Perhaps Sibyl did not tell you, but her terror
is that Basil, in spite of the Prince and the
police, may contrive to make his escape from
Russia. And if he does, how is he to live?
The Prince won't supply him with money,
certainly; and he would not like to be dependent on Sibyl—that is to say, on Sibyl's
husband. He would not mind, perhaps,
being dependent on his wife for a time.'

Narka threw out her arms, and caught the
small figure to her heart.

'Oh, Marguerite, what a blessed little
Solomon you are!' she exclaimed, in delight.
'That would indeed be a joyful culmination
—to rescue Basil from poverty and depend-
ence, and to be revenged on those who have
been so cruel to us both!'

'Oh, never mind the revenge, Narka!'
Marguerite entreated. This was not the
feeling she had meant to excite; but discussing with Narka was like stirring the
embers of a smouldering fire; the flame
leaped up and the sparks flew out when you
least expected it.

The bell rang, and Marguerite had to say good-bye and hurry off to her duties.

Narka went straight to the Rue St. Dominique. She found Sibyl in high excitement.

'Zampa has been here, and he is beside himself with satisfaction! He draws such a horoscope for you as must make all the Malibrans pine with envy in their graves. Narka, you have a splendid career before you. I am so happy! It takes such a load off my heart!'

She kissed Narka, and then turned to look at the practical side of the affair. The impresario was liberal as a prince. Narka was to proceed without delay to Florence, and put herself in training under the great master there. The whole tenor of her life was changed in an hour; she was lifted from poverty, obscurity, and carking care to ease, brilliancy, and the prospect of immediate fame. Sibyl entered into it all with that quick sympathy and subtle understanding that were part of her power.

'But you take it all too coldly, Narka,' she

said suddenly, her keen perception detecting the lack of response in Narka. 'Are you not glad, dear? I thought you would be so excited.'

'I suppose I ought to be.' Then, after a moment, 'Does M. de Beaucrillon say anything about it?' Narka asked irrelevantly.

'Gaston? He is delighted. Did you think he would not care?'

'Oh no! he is too kind not to care.' Narka repressed a sigh. She seemed tired; but there was something on her mind, Sibyl suspected. 'I am just wondering whether it will make any difference when I am before the footlights,' she said, with a constrained laugh—'whether you will feel quite the same to me when I am a public singer.'

'As if that could make the smallest difference!' Sibyl exclaimed, looking at her in blank amazement.

Narka laughed again in the constrained way.

'No doubt,' she said to herself, 'I shall remain just as far beneath the Comtesse de

Beaucrillon, *née* Princess Zorokoff, whether I turn public singer, or remain in my native obscurity as Narka Larik.'

So it was settled that they were to close at once with the impresario's offer. Narka sat down at Sibyl's table, and wrote a note saying she would prepare at once to start for Florence, and enter on her preparation for the opera. Then, to Sibyl's disappointment, she insisted on going home, alleging that she was tired and wanted rest.

Sibyl saw that she was both excited and depressed. 'You are quite feverish,' she said, holding Narka's hand, and then touching her hot forehead; 'you ought to stay here, and let me put you lying down, and bathe your temples with eau-de-cologne.'

But Narka would not be persuaded, although she would gladly have lain down, and the touch of Sibyl's cool soft hand on her aching head would have been soothing.

CHAPTER III.

DR. SCHENK IN ATTENDANCE ON NARKA.

ARKA was in a glow of heat when she left Sibyl's warm rooms, and met the bitter wind that blew hard from the north. It was a long walk and a bleak one by the river, but she faced it with a kind of reckless desperation. She reached home very tired, and was scarcely indoors when she was seized with a shivering fit.

'Mademoiselle has taken a chill,' said Eudoxie ; 'I must make her a tisane.'

The tisane did not prove as potent as Eudoxie expected. Narka spent a restless night, and in the morning her throat was swollen, her head ached and her hands burned.

'Mademoiselle has fever. I had better go to the chemist and ask him for something to cut it,' said Eudoxie.

But Narka took a pencil and wrote a line to Marguerite, and desired the maid to take it at once to La Villette.

As Eudoxie was going out with the note she met Ivan Gorff, and told him on what errand she was bound.

'Mademoiselle Narka must see a doctor at once,' he said. 'I will go and fetch one while you take that message to La Villette.'

Eudoxie gave him the key of the apartment, and hurried off to the omnibus.

Ivan called a cab and drove straight to Dr. Schenk's lodgings, and was back with him before Eudoxie had returned.

Schenk knocked at the bedroom-door; there was no answer, so he opened it and looked in. Narka was alarmed and amazed on seeing so unexpected a visitor walk into her room; but he calmed her at once by his manner as much as by his words, and ex-

plained how he came there, felt her pulse,
and, without troubling her with useless questions, withdrew. The visit did not last three
minutes, and nothing could have been more
discreet and professional than his manner
throughout.

When he went back to the salon, Marguerite was there, talking to Ivan Gorff.
She was horrified to find that the vivisector
had been called in, but she kept this to herself; he had the reputation of being a skilful
doctor, and there was comfort in that.

'What is the matter?' she inquired, when
Schenk had closed the door of the bedroom.

'Inflammation of the lungs; it has advanced very rapidly; she is in high fever.'

'Is she delirious?'

'She will be in a few hours, I expect.'

Marguerite uttered an exclamation of distress, and went into the bedroom. Narka
signed to her to stoop down.

'Go to the trunk behind the door,' she
whispered; 'you will find an ivory casket;

the key is in the drawer of the writing-table. Take it away and keep it safe for me, or for Basil.'

' It is safe enough where it is, darling,' said Marguerite ; ' I will see that nobody touches it.'

' But if anything happens to me——'

' You mean if you died ? You have not the smallest intention of doing anything so sensible,' said Marguerite, in her bright way ; ' you have caught a bad cold, and I am going to look after you till you get well. Our sisters here in the parish will come and see you every day. I'm going to tell them ; so between us you have small chance of escaping to heaven.'

Narka made an effort to say something, but her throat seemed to close, she could only form the word with her lips :

' Sibyl ?'

' I will let her know you are not well.'

Marguerite smoothed the pillow and the counterpane, and kissed Narka on the fore-head ; she then drew the curtain so as to darken the room, and went back to the salon.

During her absence, Dr. Schenk and Ivan had settled it between them that no one who understood Russian should be allowed near Narka, lest in her delirium she should betray secrets that might work mischief to herself and others.

When Marguerite reappeared, Schenk said :

' I think it right to tell you, ma sœur, that I see symptoms which threaten diph- theria ; the disease has not taken that character so far, but it may develop it before to-morrow morning ; in that case it will be necessary to find a nurse who is not afraid of the contagion. I have one whom I can trust.'

' Our sisters will take care of her,' Mar- guerite replied. ' I was going to write to Madame de Beaucrillon,' she said, turning to Ivan ; ' but if there be any fear of diphtheria she must not come.'

' It would be a great imprudence to expose

her to the risk, especially as there is no
necessity for it,' Ivan replied.

Marguerite determined to keep Sibyl away.

It proved a wise precaution as regarded
Narka. She was soon delirious, and raved
incessantly about Basil, about Kronstadt,
about Ivan and his revolutionary work ; she
talked chiefly in Russian, but now and then
she spoke in French, and Marguerite, who
very quickly detected the fiction that kept
Sibyl away, understood enough of Narka's
wanderings to make her grateful to Schenk
for inventing it.

Sibyl was unremitting in her inquiries,
and sent every day to know if there was
nothing she could do to help. Meantime
the illness, inflammation of the lungs, ran its
course without complications ; the danger
remained throughout potential, not going
beyond the peril which must attend every
serious attack of the kind. M. de Beaucrillon,
having once heard the word diphtheria pronounced, would not hear of his wife's going
near the house until Narka should have been

pronounced convalescent, and until the atmosphere should have been purified of every
lingering possibility of contagion. It was
arranged that as soon as the doctor approved
of it, Narka should come to the Rue St.
Dominique, and remain there until she went
down to Beaucrillon with the family. All
this was settled without reference to Narka
herself, her acquiescence in Sibyl's wishes
being taken for granted. She was going on
very satisfactorily, but just as the day for
her removal approached, the baby fell ill with
croup. After a week of mortal terror and
suspense to the parents, the child recovered,
but was ordered off at once to waters in
Germany. Narka consequently received a
note from Sibyl full of despair at the double
disappointment, and entreating her to go
down to Beaucrillon as soon as she felt equal
to the move, and wait there until they re-
joined her.

It would have been a great surprise to
Sibyl if she could have heard Narka exclaim,
on reading this note, 'What a relief!'

She had been looking forward with dread to the long term of close companionship with Sibyl. Weak as she was now, her one desire was to be left quiet. It would have taxed both her moral and physical strength too severely to be shut in with Sibyl, to be obliged to undergo her effusive tenderness and respond to it, and to hear her outpourings of anger and despair about Basil. Once again the blessed baby had come like a messenger of mercy to her rescue.

CHAPTER IV.

NARKA AT LA VILLETTE.

ARKA, white as an alabaster statue, and all eyes, was sitting up in her pretty salon, looking out at the old garden, and listening to the birds singing, when Marguerite came in, bringing, as usual, fresh air from heaven with her.

'I was just thinking of you,' said Narka.

'That was a very good and wholesome thought,' said Marguerite.

'Yes ; and I was wishing I was a dog.'

'That thought was not so good.'

'I was thinking that I must leave this apartment in a week, and I don't know under the broad face of heaven where to find another. Now if I were a dog, I might lodge under the stars, which would be pleasant enough, as the warm weather is at hand ; but as I am a human being, the police would take me up. As I went on thinking, it occurred to me that I might find a lodging at La Villette cheaper than in this part of the city. Do you think I could get anything clean and cheap near you ?'

Marguerite considered a moment.

'Madame Blaquette has rooms to let at the corner of the Place ; they are cheap and bright, and they take in a good bit of sky, and they are not five minutes from us.'

'Then Madame Blaquette's rooms are just the thing for me !'

A week after this conversation, Narka was installed at Madame Blaquette's.

Madame Blaquette was a character in her way. She had been servant in a gentleman's family till she was forty, and now lived by letting these rooms that took in a good bit of sky. She posed for the decayed gentle-woman. She had had a bachelor uncle, a

grocer, whose money she had always expected to inherit; and, being blessed with a
lively imagination, she had enjoyed the in-
heritance almost as much in prospect as if
she already possessed it.   She felt, therefore,
deeply wronged when, at the age of sixty,
this bachelor uncle took to himself a wife,
and, dying at the end of a year, left all he
had to her and her baby.   Madame Blaquette
always alluded to the event as 'the loss of
my fortune,' and would heave a sigh when
speaking of 'the days before my reverses.'

'She is a sentimental old goose,' said
Marguerite, 'but honest as the sun.   And
her lodgers are always respectable; they
are generally friends of mine.'

Narka had not yet discovered that to be a
friend of Marguerite's was a title to respecta-
bility open to discussion; it was not long,
however, before she became aware that Marguerite was on intimate terms with all the
waifs and strays and drunkards of the district.   For Narka, being curious to make
acquaintance with the neighbourhood, and

having as yet no work to do, went about occasionally with Marguerite on her rounds. In this way she came soon to see the influence Marguerite exercised, and the position she held, in spite of her youth—perhaps, indeed, because of it—both with her sisters and with the population of La Villette. It was very amusing to see how she queened it over them, tripping along in her heavy shoes, carrying a bundle or a basket like any little peasant-woman. The children left their play to pull at her gown and get a pat on the head ; women at their wash-tubs stopped soaping or scrubbing to exchange a word with her, or call out some piece of domestic news ; shopkeepers in the act of selling turned to nod and say, ' Bonjour, ma sœur '; *gamins* and roughs suspended their wrangling, and waited till she had passed to finish their oaths. It took Narka's breath away to see the refined, delicate girl walk up to a group of quarrelling men or boys, and order them to the right-about as if they had been children in her school. And the horny-

handed ouvrier who had spent his week's
earnings at the cabaret would take the pipe
out of his mouth and listen meekly while she
gave him a good scolding. There was something of the mother in the genial cruelty with
which she looked them in the face and said
the hard thing to them, and told them they
made her ashamed, or angry, or sorry. Her
anger would be very hot, but it never took
the form of cold displeasure; she abhorred
cold, cruel cold that hatches hate, the least
touch of whose icy breath is more fatal to
love than the hottest blast of anger. Marguerite's sympathy was an open fountain,
always flowing; when the poor went to her
with a grievance, she waxed so indignant
with them that they felt themselves avenged;
when they took her a sorrow, she pitied them
so tenderly that they left the sting of it
behind them.

One day, after a long morning of hard
work in the dispensary and the school, Narka,
who was going out with her on a round of
sick visits, said :

'What a tiring life it is that you lead, Marguerite! Do you never weary of it?'

'Never for a minute!' was the unhesitating reply. 'That is the happiness in God's service: it may tire one's body, but it keeps one's heart merry.'

'I wish I could think the poor were grateful to you,' said Narka.

'Who says they are not grateful?' demanded Marguerite quickly.

'It seems to me everybody says it; it is the constant complaint of all the good people who work for the poor that they get no return.'

'What nonsense! I wonder what sort of return they expect? If they gave love, the poor would give them love back; but they only give alms, and I don't suppose they expect the poor to give them back alms? It is so silly of people to be always looking for gratitude, and then to go about complaining that they don't get it: the disappointment sours themselves, and the complaining sours other people, for nine people out of ten are

ungrateful, and the complaining hits home
and hurts their self-love.'

Narka was amused at this touchiness con-
cerning the poor which Marguerite displayed
on the slightest provocation. They were
passing by a public-house at the moment.
A sound of voices raised high in altercation
came through the closed door.

'I do believe that is Antoine Drex that I
hear!' said Marguerite. She stood to listen,
and at the same moment the door opened,
sending out a villainous whiff of alcohol and
tobacco, and there stood Antoine Drex,
bumper aloft, apostrophizing the company.

'Ah! this is how you keep your promise,
Antoine Drex!' Marguerite called out from
the street.

The big black-bearded man stared open-
mouthed, as if the small figure in the door-
way had been the ghost of his dead wife.
A loud laugh from the spectators showed
their sense of the comical side of the tableau.

'They look drunk; come away,' said
Narka, under her breath.

But Marguerite held her ground intrepidly.
'Come out at once, and go home to your
poor old mother,' she called out to the culprit,
who stood sheepishly clutching his bumper
on the counter; 'she is very suffering this
morning, and you ought to be helping her
instead of drinking here.'

To Narka's amazement, the stalwart
man, who might have crunched up Marguerite with a finger and thumb, came out
of the cabaret like a docile dog, and walked
on before her. He looked dangerous enough,
Narka thought, for he had been drinking
copiously; this was clear from his red eye-
balls and swaggering gait, as with clenched
hanging hands he tramped up the street
before them, growling confidentially to the
paving-stones.

'Is that the man you wanted them to
guillotine?' Narka asked, when Antoine was
beyond hearing.

'Yes. How I wish they had! He would
have been safe in purgatory now, instead of
getting drunk at the Chat Botté. Those ten

months they kept him in prison before the trial put a heart of rage into the poor fellow that will get him into trouble some day. And it is hard, for the rage is only suffering in disguise. It nearly always is with the poor. Antoine would not hurt anybody. He is so good to his mother! Even when he is drunk he never touches her. And he often shares his crust with a neighbour poorer than himself. If I only could keep him out of the wine-shop!'

'The wine-shop is the bane of the poor everywhere,' said Narka.

'It is their resource, God help them! They drink to drown misery. I do believe he is trying to give me the slip, and steal into some other cabaret!' She quickened her step until Antoine turned the right corner and was out of sight. 'Ah, he is gone home,' she said, in a tone of relief. 'There is not another wine-shop between this and his lodging.'

Life at La Villette was altogether a strange experience to Narka. At first the aspect of

the place, its sordid ugliness, was so offensive
to her taste as to be a positive suffering ; but
she soon discovered that this suffering had its
compensations ; underlying the ugliness that
revolted and distressed her, there was a
hidden beauty, grander, nearer to the true
ideal than the æsthetic one that she missed ;
then the laborious courage of the population,
the kindness that springs from a sense of
common privation and mutual need, made an
atmosphere wholesome and genial at once ;
the open acceptance of a hard lot, and the
spectacle of general poverty unredeemed by
any prospect of escape, made her own lot
seem less cruel. She felt, too, more in-
dependent and secure at La Villette than she
had ever done at Chaillot or in the Faubourg
St. Germain. Here she came and went un-
molested; there was nothing shocking to
public opinion in a young girl's walking out
alone. The utter unworldliness of the place,
the absence of any necessity for keeping up
appearances, was in itself a rest. In the early
morning she went out on her little household

errands, and carried home her bread and her
can of milk, or her little basketful of marketing,
and the workmen's wives and daughters, bent
on similar errands, wished her good-morning.

As she walked through the slums, where
she was like no other inhabitant of the place,
the people, struck by her stately bearing, her
beautiful pale face, with the great eyes and
the shining hair, used at first to watch her out
of sight as if she had been some strange bird
of gaudy plumage flitting through their dark
region, and brightening it for a moment. But
in a little while they ceased even to do this.
' L'amie de ma sœur Marguerite ' soon estab-
lished her right of citizenship, and the title
was a passport to everybody's goodwill.

Narka had pledged her word to Dr.
Schenk that she would not attempt to sing
for a month from the date of her recovery.
Singing lessons were therefore out of the
question. In the meantime some of her
former pupils were taking German lessons.
These gave her a crust of bread, and, what
was almost as necessary, they kept her

occupied. For she was terribly lonely—
more lonely than she had ever been
amidst the snow-fields of Yrakow. There,
she had her mother ; but she was quite
alone now. It was a good thing that the
struggle for bare life left her little time to
brood. For body and soul must be kept
together, the fire must be lighted, the bit of
food must be cooked, the room must be
swept, her shabby clothes must be kept
mended, whether Basil was faithful or not,
whether Father Christopher was being
beaten or not, whether the Prince was
cruel or relenting. And in the interval of
home toil there were the lessons. These
German lessons were no pleasure to her,
as the singing lessons had been. They were
a mere drudgery, and she was longing for the
end of the month to set her free to sing, not
alone for the sake of the lessons, but because
the exercise of her glorious powers was in
itself an enjoyment. There was only one
more week now to wait. Then the period of
dumbness would have expired.

Signor Zampa had gone away in despair on hearing of the illness which had so suddenly fallen like a thunderbolt on his brilliant scheme. He had, however, assured Sibyl that the engagement should hold good for next season, and that as soon as Narka was well enough to enter on her preparatory studies, he should expect her to set out for Florence.

CHAPTER V.

NARKA EXPOUNDS THE GOSPEL OF THIS WORLD.

MARGUERITE was in the dispensary, measuring and mixing herbs from two green canisters, when Narka came hurriedly in, and going up to her, laid a hand on her arm; she seemed too agitated to speak.

'What is the matter? what has happened?' Marguerite asked, dropping her little shovelful of herbs back into the canister.

'I have lost it! it is gone, clear gone!' Narka gasped.

'The ivory box? Basil's papers? Oh!'

'No, my voice. I have lost it! I can't sing a note.'

She sat down, almost letting herself fall
into a straw chair.

Marguerite clasped her hands.

'When did you discover that it was gone?'

'Just now—not half an hour ago.   I had
promised not to sing a note until the month
was out.   Yesterday was the last day, and
this morning I went to the piano.   Not a
note would come.   Oh, it is too dreadful!
too dreadful!'

Marguerite, with an answering despair in
her face, stood silent, her hands still clasped.

Narka looked up, and saw the sweet brown
eyes filling with tears; she bent forward,
and let her head drop against Marguerite's
arm.

'Oh,' she said, 'what a weary burden life
is!   If one might but escape from it!'

Marguerite put her arms round her, and
held her clasped, making a little swaying
movement, as if she were rocking a child.

'It is, darling,' she said softly, after a
moment's silence; 'it *is* very weary; but we
are not carrying it alone.   There is One

under the burden with us whose help can never fail.'

Narka felt the loving breast heave under her head, and then two hot tears fall upon her cheek. If Marguerite was so full of pity, why was Marguerite's God so cruel?

'Perhaps it is not so bad as you think,' said Marguerite presently, her sunny hopefulness and practical sense coming quickly to the relief. 'After all, it may be only a temporary loss of voice. I knew a case like that in a young chorister whom we had to nurse after a typhoid fever; his voice went for some months, and he was in despair; but it came back. You must see a specialist. There is Dr. X——, who comes to the infirmary here on Tuesday; he is a great authority on the lungs and the throat. I will speak to Sœur Jeanne and ask her to arrange for you to see him here after his visit to the infirmary.'

This practical suggestion was just the touch that Narka wanted to lift her up from the torpor of despair into which the shock had thrown her. She talked it over with Marguerite, asked questions about the chorister's case, and if Marguerite strained the facts a trifle to sustain the hope they pointed to, the sin was certainly not written down against her by the recording angel. Narka went away wonderfully comforted.

The community were at once interested in her trouble. The children were all set praying for Sœur Marguerite's friend, and everyone in the house awaited with anxious curiosity to hear what Dr. X—— would say.

They had not long to wait. This was Saturday. On Tuesday morning the consultation took place. The result confirmed Marguerite's sanguine view. Dr. X—— was of opinion that the loss of the voice was likely to be only temporary : the organs were weakened by the severe inflammation they had suffered, and rest and care would in time restore their powers. If Narka had had change to the country and proper care during the period of convalescence, the accident would most likely have been avoided. She was now to think as

little about it as possible, to take any amusement within her reach, and to follow his
treatment carefully, and he promised that
before long her voice would be as fine as ever.

This verdict was received with joy by the
whole community, to whom it was at once
communicated by the Sister Superior. Marguerite was almost as thankful as Narka, and
much more demonstrative in her satisfaction,
for she already believed, while Narka still
only dared to hope.

'I wish you could have some recreation,
something to take your mind off trouble and
worry,' she said, as she and Narka sat
together in the parlour after the consultation.
'What a pity Sibyl is away! And she won't
stop in Paris on her way from Biarritz to
Carlsbad, it seems ; that is, she will only just
rest for the night.'

'I am very thankful to her for keeping out
of the way,' said Narka ; 'it was irksome as
well as odious to me to have to play the
hypocrite with her. And what else can I do
now ?'

There was no denying this.

'I almost wish it were the winter that was at hand, and not the summer,' Marguerite said; 'then your old pupils would be coming round you, and you would have your pleasant little gatherings, as you used to have at Chaillot.'

Narka laughed.

'I am not so silly as to expect anything of that sort up here. I told you before that I knew my value.'

'Your value? What do you mean? The people who were fond of you in one place would be fond of you in another, I suppose?'

'Yes, if they ever *had* been fond of me. But you don't suppose the people who came after me at Chaillot and made a fuss over me were fond of me?'

'Then why did they come after you and make a fuss over you?'

Narka laughed again.

'You heavenly little dunce! You don't know the A B C of the gospel of this world. You have never opened its catechism. You don't know that contempt of poverty is the negative side of purse-pride, and that to patronize poverty is one of the amusements of the rich. You are a dunce in snobbishness; you know nothing about the vulgarities of well-bred people and the cruelties of pious people. Fond of me! Poor dears! they were fond enough of me to turn in and spend a pleasant half-hour on their way to the Bois; but they would not drive up to this shabby place to see me. I'm not worth it.'

'Then you have no loss in such butterfly friends,' said Marguerite; 'there are better ones in store for you, please God. One must always reckon on the generous chances of life.'

'The generous chances of life!' Narka repeated, with a light laugh that was very acid; 'the generous chances of life never come to those who want them. I have found that out before this.'

'I will not have you turning sour, and looking only at the bad side of life and human beings,' said Marguerite.

'I cannot help it; my poverty hides the other side from me. But if it shuts the light out on one side, it lets it in on the other, and shows the flaws in human beings as a magnifying-glass shows the animalculæ in a drop of water. When you are poor, you see the world as it really is, with its meannesses and its vulgarities and its cruelties; people don't take the trouble to wear a mask before you; you are not worth it; it does not matter if you see the seamy side of their character; but they must take pains to make it show fair to society. My rich pupils and their mothers fancied the lessons were all on one side; they were mistaken: they taught me quite as much of their arts as I them of mine.'

'All this may be very clever and sarcastic,' said Marguerite, 'but it strikes me it is morbid, and not very charitable. It is of no use to discover our neighbours' faults unless it helps us to correct our own. There is the bell! I must go to the children's singing class.'

'I wish you would take me in hand, Marguerite, and correct me and make me good!' said Narka. 'I should like to be one of your orphans, and sit·on a bench, and have you to teach me to sing canticles, and scold me when I was naughty.'

'I'm afraid I should be scolding you from morning till night,' said Marguerite, tossing her head; 'you would never obey me without wanting to know the why and the wherefore of everything.'

She put the canisters in their place, and hurried off to the singing-class.

Narka watched her crossing the court, her step so brisk, her whole air breathing the content of a life brimful of glad activities.

'Why cannot I have a vocation,' Narka thought, 'and join these brave women, and make my life a service of love for humanity?'

She sighed; but she went home with a lightened heart, as she generally did from Marguerite's companionship.

CHAPTER VI.

THE DOWNWARD STEP.

ON reaching home Narka saw a man standing in the dark entry with the bell-rope of her door in his hand. At the first glance she did not recognise him : it was Ivan Gorff.

She uttered an exclamation of welcoming surprise, and they went in together.

'Where have you come from?' she asked excitedly, when she had closed the door.

'From everywhere.'

'Not from St. Petersburg?'

'St. Petersburg is somewhere, is it not?' Ivan said, and his face, that looked very haggard, was momentarily brightened by one of his old frank smiles.

Narka saw there was no bad news, so she inquired after his health. He shrugged his shoulders, as if the question were not worth either asking or answering.

'I saw Basil a fortnight ago,' he said, taking compassion on her; 'he is well, and he is growing in wisdom; I might almost say in grace, for he has taken the line of trying to circumvent the Prince by playing a waiting game, begging for time, and laying aside the defiant tone he had been fool enough to adopt a few months ago. So there is an end to Kronstadt.'

'Thank heaven for that!' said Narka; 'but when is there going to be an end of —the rest, I wonder? When will he be free? Will he ever be free?'

Ivan smiled, rubbed his palms together, and bent closer to her.

'I will tell you a secret,' he said, dropping his voice to a confidential undertone; 'there is a talk of the Emperor coming to pay a

visit to his good brother of Berlin, and
Prince Zorokoff is to accompany him, leaving
Basil behind, well watched, of course; but
we may outbid him, or we may outwit the
police. I have a plan——' He chuckled,
and squeezed his flattened hands between
his knees as if he would have crushed them.

Narka held her breath; she could hardly
trust herself to clutch at this splendid hope.

'Yes,' Ivan continued, enjoying the effect
he was producing; 'we must smuggle him
out across the Austrian frontier; then he
will be safe; let them catch him if they can!
It has been a good thing, this time he has
spent at St. Petersburg; it has opened his
eyes, and fitted him for the work that has to
be done. When he was called back and put
into a court dress he was in despair. He
said: "I had rather they sent me to Siberia
to work naked at the gold picking! If one
must be a slave, it is better to be naked than
to be in livery; naked, one is nearer to
being a man." But it was a good thing
they put him in livery; it made him feel

how the livery galls and pinches and degrades a man ; it has made him believe what he heard. He now knows what a devil's workshop a court is. He has seen what an open door into hell it is. He now sees that the only thing to do is to burn it down, and scatter the dust of it to the winds of heaven. He has carried the war into the enemy's country ; he has done wonders for the cause : his brain is a forge where the iron is made hot, and his pen a hammer that beats it and sends the sparks flying in every direction ; his hand has grown strong and his nerves tough, and his arm knows where to reach.'

Ivan clenched his own hand and straightened out his massive arm threateningly. He had grown excited as he went on, till his voice was hoarse, and murderous hate was visible in every line of his haggard face, and he was horrible to look at.

Narka knew not what to make of it. The sudden outbreaking of fierce passion was the more startling from its contrast with his habitual quiet *bonhomie;* she had never

dreamed of such fires smouldering beneath
the surface of Ivan's gentle nature ; she admired the strength that it revealed, but she
was conscious of a recoil from him ; a kind of
chill horror crept over her, as if she were
being forced into tacit complicity with some
criminal conspiracy, or some deed of blood.

He, concentrated in his own passion, had
not noticed its effect upon her ; but her long
silence, after he had done speaking, recalled
him to himself.

' Tell me about you,' he said, turning to
her, and his countenance changed suddenly,
as if he had thrown off a disfiguring mask.
' Why did you come to this out-of-the-way
place ?   What are you doing up here ?'

She answered his inquiries by giving him
the history of all that had happened since
they met ; for he had left Paris just as she
was pronounced out of danger ; he had
heard of her recovery from Schenk ; but
beyond that he knew nothing.

' You are with us at heart,' he said, when
she had finished ; ' why not be with us in

action ?   You said you were ready for any work that your hands or head could do.'

'What work can they do?' Narka asked, in vague alarm.

'You could translate for us.   Instead of starving on the drudgery of lessons, you might earn an easy livelihood by translating our circulars and pamphlets from Russian and German into French.   We can pay well for good service, and I could keep you supplied with work.'

He plunged his hand into a capacious breast-pocket, pulled out a roll of manuscript, unfolded it, and deliberately flattened it out on his knee.

Narka suddenly changed colour.

'That is Basil's writing!' she cried, putting out her hand to seize the paper.

'It is his writing, and it is his composition. I risked my head in travelling with it.   If it had been found, it would have been as good as a charge of dynamite under my chair.'

He handed her the paper.

Narka devoured the well-known writing

with hungry eyes ; it was almost like seeing Basil himself, like touching his hand.

Ivan's face, as he watched her, reflected transparently the battle of courage against pain that was being fought out within him ; his brow contracted, while a smile of infantine hilarity made his eyes shine. After watching her for a moment he looked away, as if he could bear it no longer.

'There is to be a meeting on the 15th,' he said, fumbling in his pockets, 'and I want to have that ready to distribute at it ; so set to work and translate it at once. By the way, why should not you come to this meeting ? You would learn something of what is being done ; you would hear what Basil is doing, and see the position he holds among us.'

'I should like greatly to go,' Narka said, looking up from the manuscript with a certain hesitation.

Her will was, in truth, pulled by opposite forces of terror and desire ; she longed to be useful in the cause for which Basil was risk-

ing his life and liberty, but she shrank before
the mystery that hung like a black curtain
between her and the means and agencies it
employed. Who were these people she was
going to associate herself with? Despera-
does, probably, who shrank from nothing.
Still, if they were Basil's fellow-workers——

'I will come and fetch you,' said Ivan, his
quick eye detecting the conflict in her mind;
'we can go in together, and you can come
away whenever you feel inclined. We shan't
be more than a few score.'

And so it was settled that she would go.

CHAPTER VII.

THE MEETING IN THE QUARTIER LATIN.

THE meeting was to be held in the Quartier Latin, close to the Russian Library. On the appointed evening Ivan called for Narka, and they drove there in a cab. It drew up before an old-fashioned gateway, and Ivan led the way up a dark, slippery stair to an entresol, where they entered a low-ceiled room lighted with gas. The artificial glare, after the golden light of the summer evening, had a sinister effect, and lent an additional air of mystery to the place and the opportunity, which impressed Narka's excited imagination.

There were about a dozen persons already present, some of them women. Every eye was turned on her, and the women looked eager to claim acquaintance ; but Ivan Gorff, after exchanging greetings with the men he knew, sat down beside her, placing his chair so as to barricade her against approach, and then engaged her in confidential talk. The room filled quickly. Still they seemed to be waiting for some one who had not yet arrived. Presently the door opened, and Dr. Schenk appeared.

It was not a pleasant surprise to Narka ; but it was not as disagreeable as it might have been under other circumstances. She did not like Schenk, though she was grateful to him, with limitations, for the care he had taken of her in her illness ; but she was glad to see him make his way round and take a seat beside her. His presence seemed a protection. Never had she found herself amidst such an assembly of vulgar, vicious, desperate-looking human beings as those who composed this meeting. The first impression of mistrust was gradually giving way to one of horror and amazement.

They were all talking at the top of their voices, gesticulating in an excited manner ; they seemed to be discussing every subject under the sun, if incoherent remarks and wild rant could be called discussion ; it was difficult to believe such an assembly could have any serious purpose in view, or that the members were capable of wise and con-certed action. When it was ascertained that the meeting was full, the door was locked, and someone stamped on the floor, and then knocked on the table, and clamoured for silence in order that the speaking might begin.

The first speaker was an elderly Russian, a tall, massively built man, with a quantity of black beard growing all over his face, and through which his sharp, rat-like eyes and exceedingly red nose peered like live things through a jungle. He read some reports from distant members, scarcely intelligible to Narka, but evidently of interest to the

company. The speaker alluded proudly to
his having been fifteen years at the hulks—a
fact which evidently gave him a standing, as
one entitled by experience to hold a heavy
brief against the tyrants. The time had
come, he said, for overturning that great
collective tyrant called Society, and the
work demanded stout hearts and steady
hands. The stamping and applause which
emphasized this remark left no doubt as to
the readiness of the hearts and hands of the
company.

'Those,' continued the speaker, when
quiet was restored, 'who possess what by
right belongs to humanity call our work
crime, and hunt us down. But if we are
guilty, who are the true criminals? If our
deeds are bloody, on whose head will be the
blood we shed? They goad us to madness,
and when we strike in self-defence they call
us robbers and assassins; they murder us in
the name of justice!'

The old convict went ranting on in the
same style, his voice growing louder as he

proceeded, until it reached a shout ; his gestures, at first heavy and emphatic, grew rapid and vehement, till his Herculean arms leaped and lashed about like the wings of a mill blown this way and that by contrary winds.

Ivan Gorff joined in the general applause, laughing and clapping hands as if the whole thing had been a clever farce. Schenk sat with his arms crossed, impassive and silent.

The next speaker represented a very different type. He also was Russian, but young (about thirty), with a battered, consumptive countenance, and faded blond colouring. He was nobly born, had ruined himself by gambling, and been driven from sheer want into the business of patriotism ; but he attributed his misfortune to the evil influences of the court (he had once succeeded in getting an invitation to a state ball at the Winter Palace), and felt that his mission was to denounce the foul corruption of courts and the vices of kings, and to serve the noble cause of revolution by holding himself up as

an awful example. He was interrupted by
fits of coughing, and the intervals were filled
with frantic applause from the meeting.

'It is some consolation to know,' he continued, 'that others are carrying on the war
in the very heart of the citadel, and fighting
in the foul atmosphere of courts against those
infernal agencies. One of our countrymen
is giving a glorious example of self-sacrifice
and courage in propagating the gospel of
hate under the roof of the tyrant, and mining
the ground under his feet. My friend and
heroic brother in arms, Basil Zorokoff——'

A faint, inarticulate cry from a corner of
the room was instantly drowned in a loud
and prolonged burst of applause from Ivan
Gorff, and this was the signal for a general
storm of enthusiasm, before which the consumptive speaker, already exhausted, collapsed.

The hubbub might have lasted indefinitely,
if Schenk had not risen, and, with one hand
in his breast, and the other uplifted to command silence, made evident his intention to

speak. The effect was immediate. The clamorous tongues were hushed, and silence reigned in the room. Schenk spoke with a quiet power that was impressive; his accent was slightly German; his voice clear and distinct; his speech simple and direct, like that of a man who is too sure of the strength of his subject to care to borrow any aid from rhetoric or gesticulation.

'We are a company of martyrs,' he said, 'self-elected victims in the great cause of Humanity. Let every man keep this grand ideal well before him. Our duty is to annihilate self in the service of the general good. The claims of the universal brotherhood must swallow up every other claim. Every creed and code and prejudice must succumb at their bidding. In the interests of our noble cause we must be ready, at midday or at midnight, to sacrifice self. We must be ready to do and to suffer things hard and vile and hideous. The men and women who join us must hold their lives in their hands, and be ready to fling them away

at an hour's notice. They must consent to
trample under foot what the world calls
honour, and to renounce the slavish superstition of its so-called moral law. They must
be strong enough to lie without blenching in
the interests of their brethren, and to strike
with a steady aim when the good of the
cause demands a tyrant's death. They must,
in a word, give their tongue for a sword, and
their right hand for a dagger, to be used
whenever the sacred cause of Humanity
demands it. They must be prepared to
suffer hunger and thirst, to endure heat and
cold, to give their flesh to the iron and the
scourge, and their good name to the dogs;
to be accursed by their kindred; to be ac-
counted infamous by the good and virtuous;
to be alone in life and in death. All this,
they who cast in their lot with us must be
ready to accept. If there be any among us
whose spirit quails before the prospect, let
him go no farther, but leave us before it is
too late. Let no man or woman who cannot
face with unflinching nerve the issues that

await us, run the risk of betraying the cause, and incurring the traitor's death.'

Schenk paused, as if waiting for an answer. It came in a loud shout of assent from every side. With a quiet gesture he imposed silence, and went on :

'If we are all sure of ourselves, we need fear nothing. No man can hurt us. They can do no more than kill us, and we are willing to be killed. However black in the eyes of men, we are white and clean before heaven and our own conscience. And we stand all equal as servants in the grand cause. The lowest among us who runs the same risks, deserves the same honour as the Prince who is working in the high places. The only standard we recognise is patriotism ; the value of each man is measured by the service he renders to the general cause.'

Schenk then proceeded to read letters and reports. But Narka did not hear them. She was reeling from the blow that his speech had dealt her; she felt like a person who had been led blindfold into a quagmire, and who, when

the bandage was removed, saw no way out of
it. What could Ivan's motive have been in
leading her into such a place? He had,
indeed, prepared her vaguely by mysterious
hints; but she never dreamed of anything so
reckless of morality as this policy expounded
by Schenk. And it looked as if Schenk
had seized with avidity the opportunity of
lighting up the depths of the abyss on the
brink of which she stood, and showing her
what kind of solidarity she incurred and what
risks she ran in throwing in her lot with him
and his associates. And these men were
Basil's friends! It was impossible! Yet
there was his pamphlet. . . . True, it did not
contain anything like Schenk's cold-blooded
gospel of crime; it was only an eloquent
appeal to his countrymen to rise and assert
their dignity as men, and their freedom as
citizens; it dealt with abstract ideas and
principles.

Narka in her bewilderment could not,
perhaps would not, see that Schenk's concrete
code was only the logical outcome of Basil's

abstract principles. Suddenly the thought of Larchoff flashed through her mind : she felt sick with doubt and terror.

Schenk sat down, and then Olga Borzidoff rose to speak. This woman was a friend of Dr. Schenk's, and had kept her eyes on Narka from the first with a glance which, if Narka had noticed it, would have frightened her more than anything she had seen or heard at the meeting. Olga Borzidoff, after draining the cup of pleasure to the dregs, had taken to the game of patriotism in search of a new sensation ; but she played badly, got caught, and only escaped with her life owing to a timely warning from one of the Emperor's aides-de-camp. Her fortune was confiscated, but the sale of her jewels gave her an income which enabled her to play the *grande dame* amongst the bankrupt pariahs into whose society she had sunk. She had once been handsome, but now, at forty, she was a bold, hard-featured, painted coquette.

She opened her speech by an attack on men, denouncing the despotism they exer-

cise over women, and declaring that the
emancipation of her sex must be a prelude to
the emancipation of her country and man-
kind, and that her efforts and those of her
sisters should tend in that direction.   A
violent, ranting rigmarole.

After this shrieking sister, a pale-faced,
blue-eyed German stood up. She acknow-
ledged that she was a woman, timid and
cowardly, and, therefore, had no right to put
herself forward ; still, trusting to the chivalrous indulgence of the stronger sex, she
dared to lift up her voice and adjure them to
make haste in their grand mission of social
reform.   Their action had hitherto been
circumscribed by scruples of compassion
which were in reality the promptings of
cowardice.   They shrank from sacrificing
harmless men and women, forgetting that
the death of one tyrant was such a gain to
humanity as to be cheaply bought by the
sacrifice of a thousand lives ; it would bene-
fit millions yet unborn.   Let this thought
nerve their arm for the slaughter that must

be accomplished if the world was to be cleansed of the race of tyrants and aristocrats, etc., etc., etc.

The blue-eyed woman's voice had a lachrymose tremble in it that was full of pathos. It reminded Narka of the serpent beseeching Eve to eat to the death of the human race.

Several other speakers followed, chiefly French, all young men, evidently of the *déclassé* type. One after another they stood up and raved and ranted; they were full of their own importance, ready for any enterprise, absolutely reckless of consequences; light-headed fools, seemingly more hungry and discontented than wicked; a wonderful company to undertake the redemption of their respective nations.

Ivan Gorff had not spoken, except that short parley improvised to screen Narka when she had nearly betrayed herself. He rose now, and said he had something to communicate before they separated. There was a general assent, and he proceeded to read out, in his deep, metallic voice, Basil's

pamphlet translated. The effect was electric. The language had seemed inspiring to
Narka when she read it alone; but declaimed
by Ivan to this excited and responsive
audience, its eloquence was like fire and
dancing flames. The reading was all along
punctuated by 'bravos' and suppressed
cheers. The meeting could hardly restrain
its enthusiasm within bounds, and the moment Ivan had done, the applause burst out
like a torrent let loose. The pamphlets were
seized upon as if they had been loaves of
bread thrown to starving men; the company
embraced one another; they kissed the
pamphlet; they made every demonstration
of wild delight.

Under cover of the general hubbub, Ivan
said to Narka:

'Let us slip away.'

Dr. Schenk, who was before her, moved
on at once; and Olga Borzidoff, whose eyes
had never left the group, pushed quickly
towards the door and met them.

'Present us to one another,' she said to

Schenk, putting her hand on his arm ; but
Schenk moved on as if he had not heard.
' Let us introduce ourselves,' said Olga. ' I
am Olga Borzidoff. What is our new sister's
name ?'

' Narka Larik,' replied the new sister
coldly.

Ivan pushed her gently on, remarking that
it was later than he thought. It was pitch-
dark on the stairs. Schenk struck a match,
and nursed the little flame, that Narka
might see where to step ; but the light, after
a moment, went out.

' Take my arm,' said Schenk. ' I know
the way. I will guide you.'

They were groping their way, Ivan follow-
ing, when a hand was laid on his shoulder,
and a woman's voice said :

' I want a word with you.'

He stood at her bidding.

Narka got safe down, thanks to Schenk's
steady guidance. When they emerged into
the court below the moon was high, and the
dark blue heaven was full of stars.

' Here we are, *a riveder le stelle !*' he said, drawing a deep breath.

In spite of the horror with which his speech had so lately inspired her, Narka for a moment felt in sympathy with him ; the beautiful quotation seemed to strike a *sursum corda* that lifted her spirit out of the dense atmosphere in which she had been morally and physically stifling.

They stood and looked back, expecting Ivan to follow ; but he did not appear, and the others were hurrying down.

' We had better not wait here,' said Schenk. 'Come on, and I will put you into a cab.'

They went out, and he hailed one, and assisted Narka into it. As he was closing the door upon her, he said :

' It is very late for you to go such a long drive alone ; you had better let me see you home.'

And without waiting for her answer, he jumped in beside her.

Neither of them broke silence until they

alighted at Narka's door. Then Schenk wished her good-night, and walked away in the starlight.

Narka went in and locked her door; then, throwing aside her bonnet and mantle, she opened the window wide, and began to walk up and down the room with the nervous but determined step of one who is struggling by bodily movement to escape from the lingering clutch of a nightmare.

'Good God!' she cried out loud to herself, 'has Basil adopted these devilish principles? Is he working with these men?' The thought of it made her sick. She seemed to hear that poor dissipated-looking *roué* exclaiming, 'Basil Zorokoff, my friend and brother-in-arms!' . . . Schenk's words kept sounding in her ears: 'Those who join us must be prepared to throw their good name to the dogs . . . to lie without blenching; to kill when they are commanded. . . .'

Narka took her forehead in both hands as if to crush out the thoughts that were making it burn and throb. After a while, she grew dizzy from measuring the short tether of the room, and sat down by the open window. She felt like a lonely creature caught in a trap, and shut out from all chance of rescue. Perhaps Basil felt something like this? If he had committed himself to these doctrines, and linked himself with these men, he had most assuredly been entrapped into it un-awares, just as she had been entrapped into attending the meeting to-night. What could have induced Ivan to take her there, unless he wanted to inspire her with disgust for the whole thing? And Schenk too, brutally parading before her the naked horror of the cause and the system she had blindly espoused! Was it with a view to warning her? Or was it to make her feel that she was in his power?

There was something altogether Sphinx-like about Schenk; something mysterious that by turns fascinated and repulsed her. The antipathy she felt towards him at moments amounted to positive loathing; and then again, he drew her to him by a strong compelling power, half mental, half moral; his intellectual refinement, his strength of character, his supreme, though misguided, spirit of self-sacrifice, commanded her admiration. And Basil's was just the nature to be attracted by these gifts, and to be seduced by the glamour of false heroism that Schenk threw over his monstrous theories; it sounded so sublime, this counting for nothing the failure of the individual effort, the ruin of the personal life, where the grand impersonal ambition was to be served! It all looked beautiful in the distance; but Narka had come near enough to see through the glamour into the horrible corruption that lay beneath it.

She had been dreaming all her life of a grand revolution which was to set Russia free, and sweep away the tyrannies and turpitudes that were weighing down her people. This she knew could not be accomplished without violence; but violence in a just cause was justified; bloodshedding was inevitable in every revolution. She accepted this condition in the abstract, without dwelling much on circumstance or degree; but she had never contemplated abolishing the moral law and honour and truth as 'slavish superstition.' This was diabolical. There was no cohesive element in such doctrines as these. They were murderous and suicidal; they could destroy and annihilate; but they could generate nothing. Was there, then, no outlook anywhere else? For if not, Narka saw nothing but Despair to cling to. And Despair was the door into madness. She seemed to be standing very close to that door at this moment. Her thoughts, her feelings, the past and the present, were all a tumult of chaos. Many voices were crying out in discordant strife within her, like an orchestra of instruments all attuned to different keys, and each trying to out-scream the other.

If Death, not Life, was the conquering power of this world, what was the good of struggling? Better give it up, and lie down and die at once. No efforts of mortal man

could avail against Death. And if the
creation of Humanity was a tragic failure,
all endeavours to mend it could only be a
series of failures, less fatal, but equally
barren. Such a creed was enough to drive
men mad. If it spread, Russia was fated to
become one vast madhouse. And yet the
men who held this insane creed seemed to
be the only ones who were in earnest about
life ; the only ones who believed in the re-
generation of their country, and who were
brave enough to suffer and toil for its accom-
plishment. How could they suffer without
hope, and not go mad? The wonder was
that generations of inherited despair had not
destroyed the reason of the Russian people
long ago. A still greater wonder was that it
was only now betraying their faith ; that they
had been content to bear their cruel doom
through the centuries, muttering in their
hearts, 'If God were not so high above us,
and the Czar so far away!'

It was only yesterday the people had
waked up from the lethargy of this blind

superstition, and begun to ask : ‘ Why is all
this allowed to go on ? Why should we,
millions, continue for ever tortured and down-
trodden under the reign of an omnipotent
God who claims to be the God of Mercy
and of Love ?’

This dreadful ‘ why,’ which had long been
uttering itself in Narka’s heart, was clamour-
ing in her brain now until she almost fancied
she was going mad herself. There was
neither sequence nor logic in the way the
question repeated itself, or in the answers
that arose confusedly to quiet her. She sat
on at the open window until the night air
chilled her, and the dark street grew silent
as a graveyard, and the stars faded out of
the sky. Then she shut the window, and,
shivering, threw herself on her bed, and tried
to fall asleep.

CHAPTER VIII.

GOLD IN THE DROSS.

THE meeting in the Quartier Latin had one good effect on Narka: it forced her thoughts into a new channel, and made it easier for her to obey the doctor's injunction of thinking as little as possible about her lost voice. That extraordinary scene, and the sudden and dangerous current it had introduced into her life, absorbed her so completely that all other thoughts were for the moment crowded out of sight. But she felt more alone since her solitude had become peopled by this multitude of unbidden presences. A new sense of loneliness, of isolation, came to her with

the longing to discount these too vivid
emotions, to silence these haunting revela-
tions and shadowy presentments by sharing
them with some one whom she could trust,
and who would understand, whose sympathy
or whose contradiction, whose indignant
denunciation even, might help her to adjust
the balance of things, and bring them to
their true proportion. It is so much harder
to battle through these spectral crowds
alone !

Narka tried to escape from her beleaguered
solitude by occupying herself, and being as
much as possible out of doors. One of the
few helpful recreations within her reach was
a visit to the Louvre. She took the omnibus
one morning and drove there. The serene
atmosphere of the galleries soothed her, the
brooding presence of the dead masters, who
were still so living, exorcised the evil spirits
and scared them away. She had never held
a brush, but her delight in the art was
genuine. She loved some of the pictures as
if they were living persons who felt her

enthusiasm, and might be touched by it; sometimes it almost seemed to her that she might awake, or trouble the sleep of the dead painters in being so deeply moved by their inspired renderings. She lingered long before them to-day, and though tired physically from standing about so many hours, she left the place, refreshed and rested in spirit.

She was turning into the Tuileries gardens, when a gentleman, hurrying out, met her. It was Dr. Schenk. Narka had not seen either him or Ivan Gorff since the meeting.

' I am so glad to meet you!' he said cordially; 'shall we sit down and chat for a moment ?'

There was a bench close by, under the broad shade of a chestnut-tree. Narka was not sorry to sit down and rest a little.

' I need not ask what you thought of the company the other evening,' Schenk said, entering at once on the subject.

Narka's level brows went up expressively.

'It was not so much the company, even, as the doctrines, that took me by surprise,' she answered.

'You were not prepared to find them so advanced? Ivan ought to have been more outspoken and explicit with you. You were hardly strong enough to bear the shock of being brought in contact with the reality so suddenly. I took for granted that you had come there with your eyes open, and I was surprised to see you, I confess. However, as you have been taken behind the curtain, you must just accept the fact that there is an ugly side to patriotism when it has to work in secret. But though the patriotism that goes forth to the roll of drums and the braying of trumpets looks a more respectable thing, it is far less worthy in reality than ours that gets no reward but scorn and stripes; we at least despise the conventional fallacy that goes by the name of honour; we trample that cant and the rest of the world's jugglery and caricaturing under our feet, and we bring on ourselves the odium of the

result for a purely impersonal gain. I per-
ceive you have a great deal to learn as to
our principle of action,' he added, reading,
with his habitual intuition, on Narka's
features the conflict between utter revulsion
and reluctant admiration that he was exciting
in her; 'you have taken a perilous step in
joining us, but you will trust me and let me
be your friend——'

'I hope our new sister will trust us all as
friends,' said a woman's voice behind them.

Before turning round to see who it was,
Narka had recognised Olga Borzidoff. She
started and coloured. Schenk stood up.

'What brings you here?' he said, in a
low tone that had something dangerously
fierce in it.

'Precisely what brings you here,' she
replied, in a high, insolent key; 'the desire
to converse with Mademoiselle Larik.'

'I had business to discuss with mademoiselle.'

'So have I. Perhaps you won't mind our
discussing it together?'

'Good-morning, monsieur,' said Narka, and quivering with anger and wounded pride, she walked away.

That bold, bad woman's stare was like the touch of an unclean thing. She could not forgive Ivan Gorff for subjecting her to the humiliation of such a contact. Why had he entrapped her so treacherously into this secret congregation of disreputable men and women? What sort of good were such people capable of effecting for their country? And Basil was working in common with them! . . .

All the way to La Villette, as the omnibus rolled along, Narka protested inwardly against this unworthy comradeship, and up-braided Ivan Gorff. But on reaching home she found that Ivan had called, and left a sealed parcel for her. She opened it, and saw Basil's handwriting. In an instant all her anger vanished, and she could feel nothing but gratitude towards the man who had brought this joy into her life.

She sat down and devoured the manu-

script. It was just what she wanted to
restore her wounded self-respect and recon-
cile her to the irreconcilable. The article
was a powerful and impassioned piece of
writing; but it remained, like the preceding
one, in the abstract, dealing with principles,
and enlarging on the effect of tyranny upon
the moral nature of a people. Here was
the wisdom, the sagacity, the courage, the
dominant mind of the true patriot! This
was the gold in the dross. Narka set to
work at once on the translation, happy in
the consciousness that she was putting her
hand to the plough with Basil, and driving
the share through the smoking soil, while he
cast the seed into the furrow.

CHAPTER IX.

SIBYL MAKES ACQUAINTANCE WITH LA VILLETTE.

NARKA had not been to see Marguerite since the meeting. If anyone had asked her why, she would have said it was because she had been busy, or absent at Marguerite's convenient hours for seeing her. But the true, though unacknowledged, reason was that she shrank from the contact. Marguerite's pure and uncompromising orthodoxies somehow always rebuked her like a living conscience ; and now that her mind had become tainted with guilty knowledge, and was tacitly, half-consciously, conniving at it, she did not dare intrude herself on a life filled from morning

till night with placid sanctities, sweet and
common as daisies in the grass, and wholesome as a field of new-mown hay. She was
afraid to meet those true, innocent eyes that
were bubbling up with happiness and trust in
God and man, like clear fountains in the sun-
light. She avoided Marguerite since she had
set her foot upon the downward path—for
Narka knew that it was a downward path.
Those articles of Basil's had fanned the flame
of her love and fired her imagination, but
they had not blinded her reason. She saw
clearly enough the logical link between those
blood-stirring appeals and the doctrines enun-
ciated at the meeting, so she stayed away.

Marguerite, meantime, was too busy to go
to people who were able to come to her. She
heard from Madame Blaquette that Narka
was well and out every day, and this was
enough. She had, moreover, heavier cares
than usual pressing on her for the moment.
La Villette was 'nervous'; in other words, it
was making ready for a revolution. The
elders of the Sisterhood, enlightened by past

experiences, recognised signs and symbols which Marguerite's quick intuition could not have failed, even without this warning, to notice ; the district echoed with sounds and silences that were not to be mistaken ; the wine-shops were crowded late and early, and through their closed doors there came reverberations of that alcoholic oratory which to the Parisian *ouvrier* is like a lighted match put to powder. A more significant sign to Marguerite was that the orators avoided her. She noticed that men, who habitually met her with a bright kindly word, now turned round the corner when they saw her in the distance, or, if they came up with her unexpectedly, hurried on with a curt salutation. Clearly they were fighting shy of her, and she read the reason in their sullen averted faces, and in the troubled eyes of the women.

Madame Blaquette, whom Narka frequently met coming in and out, seemed much alarmed, and hinted at some great impending catastrophe ; but Madame Blaquette was so well known as a croaker and

an alarmist that no one paid any heed to what
she said. One afternoon she came against
Narka in the entry, and clutched her arm in
great excitement.

'Oh, mademoiselle, we have had the
narrowest escape! Just think! The house
opposite is watched by the police, and such
odd-looking people have been hanging about!
Three days back, a box was brought to a
man who lodged there a month ago. They
wouldn't take it in, so the porter carried it
over here, and said if I kept it for a couple of
days it would be called for. I, never sus-
pecting anything, took it into my room, and
this morning it suddenly occurred to me that
it might be an infernal machine!'

'Oh!' cried Narka, with a gesture of
dismay.

'I went off at once to the commissaire de
police, and he went to the Préfecture, and
three men came just now and carried it into
the backyard, and took all *sorts* of precautions
in opening it, for if it had exploded, you know,
the whole street would have been blown up!'

'But it didn't explode?'

'Oh no; it was a sewing-machine. But only think if it had been the other!'

'But it wasn't the other,' said Narka, half amused, and half vexed at having been so taken in.

'All the same, we have had a most merciful escape!' insisted Madame Blaquette, 'for it *might* have been the other, and I might have been buried at this moment under the ruins of my own roof. We ought to be on our knees thanking God!'

Narka, with an impatient shrug, passed on, laughing, into her room. As she took off her things she looked out at the house opposite. It was a dingy, disreputable-looking house, with a battered face, and windows so crusted with dirt you could not have seen through them—a house that looked as if it might want watching; but probably there was as much foundation for its bad character as for the providential escape from the sewing-machine.

She was turning from the window, when

her attention was attracted by an unusual movement outside ; a number of *gamins* were rushing to stare at something ; presently an open carriage with liveried servants drew up before her door. Flushed and excited, Narka opened her door, and waited to receive Sibyl.

' Oh, my darling, what a funny place you have come to !' exclaimed Sibyl, looking round her with a bewildered air.

' Yes,' said Narka, with a constrained laugh, ' it is a funny place for you to come to pay a visit. I wonder what your servant think of it ?'

' My servants ? I should as soon think of wondering what my horses thought of it !'

Narka laughed again.

' Yes,' she said within herself, ' horses and servants are the same sort of cattle to you, only with different prices.'

They sat down, Sibyl glancing round her with a kind of half-alarmed curiosity.

' Do you know, I am very angry with you,' she said. ' What business had you to steal a march on me, and come off to this outlandish place the moment my back was turned ?'

' I was obliged to come away ; I could not remain where I was.'

' You might have gone down to Beaucrillon and waited there. Have you made a vow never to come and stay with me ?'

Narka made no answer for a moment. Then, looking at Sibyl with an expression half grave, half comical :

' Do you remember,' she said, ' how we laughed long ago over that remark of Madame de Staël's, that a woman who was unhappy with her husband ought never to leave him, because it made it so much worse for her when she had to come back to him ?'

' Where is the husband here ?' said Sibyl, glancing round as if she half expected to see him hiding somewhere ; ' have you gone and married unbeknown to me ?'

' The husband is only a figure,' replied Narka. ' The fact is, the contrast between my life and yours is too great; the charm and splendour of your home make the hurry-scurry and sordid vulgarities of my own look worse to me. I have made up my mind not to risk it, not to try to snatch at what has been so completely taken from me. It is much better for me to stay in my own corner, and toil and moil, and never try to escape and put on my silk gown and sit idle like a lady. I feel such a sham when I go to you and play the lady!'

'What nonsense you are talking! You are a sham when you try not to play the lady, as you call it. Your ladyhood is as inalienable as the shape of your eyes, or the colour of your hair. I don't know what you mean by sordid vulgarity; a life of intellectual labour is not sordid or vulgar. It has always seemed to me a grand thing to owe everything to one's self. I should have been very proud if I could have earned my own living.'

The sentiment was sublimely absurd in Sibyl's mouth, and yet it did Narka good to hear her speak so. It raised her in her own eyes to hear Sibyl say that working for bread was a grand thing. There was still a virtue in Sibyl's touch that was like nothing else.

They talked about other things, and then Sibyl said :

' And Marguerite ? You see her often ? How is she ?'

' I hope she is well, for she works like a little pony. She is goodness itself to me.'

' I am so glad, darling ! But Marguerite is an angel.'

' I knew that already ; but since I came up here I have discovered that she is a genius. She would have made a first-rate queen. She has a genius for governing. If you could see how she manages the roughs and the drunkards ! And the people positively worship her ; there are all sorts of stories abroad about the miracles Sœur Marguerite works ; how she multiplies the soup and the rations beyond all natural explanation. Where she gets the money for all she gives away in food and clothing is certainly a kind of miracle.'

'Oh, she is not a bad beggar!' said Sibyl, laughing; 'her genius extends in that direction too, I can tell you! I must go in and see her on my way home.' Then, taking Narka's hand in her own: 'But tell me about your voice, dearest?' she said anxiously. 'I have been haunted by the thought ever since I heard from Marguerite that you had lost it. How I did long to fly to you that moment, and hold your hand while you were passing through the terrible anguish of the first discovery! But it is sure to come back. Have you tried it since then?'

Before Narka could answer, there was a quick tap at the window, which was only a few feet from the ground outside, and something like a great white wing fluttered past.

'It is Marguerite!' said Narka; and, doubly glad of the interruption, she went to let her in.

The cornette seemed to bring in the sunshine with it.

'I guessed who was responsible for the scandal of a powdered flunky in this respectable neighbourhood,' said Marguerite. 'Who ever thought of your ladyship's being in town at this time of year? Business? Well, Narka is not so badly off, you see!' and she glanced admiringly round the room, in which, in spite of its tiled floor and whitewashed walls, the grand piano under its rich embroidered cover, and flowers and books about, gave a gracious, home-like air.

'If the outside were only as good as the inside! But what an awful neighbourhood it is!' said Sibyl, lifting up her hands. 'As I drove up here the wickedness of the people's faces, the way they scowled at me, made me shudder.'

'You need not have shuddered,' said Marguerite, with a little toss of her head. 'The worst of our people up here is they are not hypocrites; they wear their wickedness outside instead of in; half the time it is pain that makes them scowl, poor creatures! When hunger is griping a man's inside, it is enough to make him scowl. I'm sure it would me.'

'You always stand up for your people here,' said Sibyl, 'but you know very well, dear, they are the scum of the city.'

'I know nothing of the sort; they may be the dregs, but they certainly are not the scum —the scum is at the top. You must look to our *monde* for that.'

'We don't get drunk, at any rate.'

'Humph!' Marguerite remembered certain *traits de mœurs* she had heard at Yrakow, and admired Sibyl's impudence. 'Perhaps it would be better for them if they did,' she said defiantly. 'I know a few respectable Pharisees whom I should love to make so drunk that they would roll under the table. That might take the pride out of them, and send them up to the Temple to strike their breasts and get justified.'

Narka burst out laughing.

'The Pharisees get no quarter from Marguerite,' she said.

Sibyl looked half inclined to be angry.

'Well, if she is fond of publicans, I should think she is satisfied up here. The shouts

and yells from the wine-shops as I came
along were perfectly awful. It reminded me
of the shrieks of the damned.'

' That can't be a pleasant noise,' said Marguerite ; ' but I would rather hear that than
the laughter of the damned.'

' I did not know they ever laughed in
hell.'

' I fancy they do now and then ; I fancy
when the Pharisees are stripped of their
shams, and shown up naked at the judgment-
seat, their countenances on finding themselves
in that predicament must be a sight to make
even the poor devils laugh.'

' The poor devils ? Well, if you are going
to stand up for the devils !'

' It would be a good thing if we had their
zeal and their perseverance,' retorted Marguerite.

' You need not envy them their spirit
of contradiction, at any rate,' said Sibyl
good-humouredly, feeling that she had made
a hit.

' Give it up, Sibyl—give it up,' said Narka,

triumphing with Marguerite, who had had the best of it up to this.

But Marguerite had not thought of triumphing ; she only thought of defending her poor people.

' What news have you from St. Petersburg ?' she asked, turning the conversation.

Sibyl slowly lifted her shoulders, and, with a sigh, slowly let them down.

' I'm afraid my father is growing weak. Basil has persuaded him to wait and give him time to live down his foolish passion. I fear Basil has entangled himself deeper, and in more ways than we suspected. And he has broken through all restraint with my father, and rails against the tyranny of the Emperor and the miserable condition of the people, and goes on like a lunatic. The wonder is that my father bears it. But the wonder of all is that anyone so clever as Basil can be such a fool ! As if our moujiks wanted to be free ! As if they would know what to do with themselves if they were sent adrift to-morrow like English or French peasants! To give them perfect freedom would be to make them miserable.'

'My dear Sibyl,' Narka protested, with a laugh, 'would a lark be miserable if you opened its cage and set it free?'

'Yes, it would, if it had been born in a cage. That is what you and Basil don't consider.' (How that 'you and Basil' made Narka's heart leap!) 'Human beings, like animals, are only happy in the conditions they are born to. A savage is happy in savage conditions; our civilized ways would be misery to him. Fancy a red Indian, roaming through his forests in a bead necklace, suddenly trapped, and his free limbs packed into pantaloons and top-boots!'

'We Russians are not quite red Indians,' said Narka; 'and we have been slowly educating ourselves up to top-boots these fifty years past.'

'*Un*fortunately!' said Sibyl, with intense emphasis. 'Our people were much happier before they ever heard of top-boots. They were content with their lot, just as the camel

is content that toils all his life through the
desert ; but bring a camel up as a pet to eat
and drink and lie in the shade, and then load
him and turn him out into the desert to tramp
without water under a vertical sun, and do
you think he would be content ?'

' He would be a great fool if he were. But
what does that prove ?—that the majority
of human beings ought to be treated like
camels ?'

' They ought not to be unfitted for their
allotted work.'

' Allotted ? Who allotted it ? When God
created the world, did He allot the millions as
camels to the tens ? Did He authorize you
to treat the people as cattle ?'

' I don't think we ever treated our people
as cattle,' said Sibyl, surprised and resentful.

' *You* did not ; but others around you
did, and you might if you had chosen. I
don't believe God ever meant to place the
majority of His children in jeopardy to that
choice.'

There was a passionate vibration in Narka's

voice that bade Sibyl remember how cruelly
the choice had been used against her kindred;
the remembrance smote her heart, if not her
conscience. There was an awkward silence,
when Marguerite exclaimed:

'Good gracious! is that three o'clock? I
had only meant to stay ten minutes, and you
have beguiled me into wasting twenty! Dear
Sibyl, you will be interested to hear that I am
as poor as a rat, and ready for any spare cash
you may want to get rid of. I just mention it
in case you should not like to ask me. Now
I must be off!'

She kissed her, and hurried away.

'Where is she going in such a hurry?' inquired Sibyl, when Narka returned, after
closing the door.

'She is gone to dress the wound of a
carter whose leg was smashed under a stone,
and then amputated. It is a frightful case.
Marguerite dresses the wound twice a day.'

Sibyl shuddered.

'It is extraordinary how hard Marguerite
has grown; she can stand by without wincing,

and look on at those horrors, while the very
sight of blood makes me sick! But it is
much better for one's self and others not to
be so tender-hearted. I should think the
atmosphere of this place, with such misery
all about as Marguerite describes, must be
very bad for you, Narka, it is so depressing?
And you want to be cheered up. Now I
look at you, my darling, you seem very tired.
I am sure you are overworking yourself.
You want rest. You ought to be lying down
this minute. I wish I could stay and put you
on the sofa, and read to you for an hour.
Have you any nice books?'—she glanced
round at the table. 'When I come back I
will *insist* on your letting me take care of
you.' She stood up, and looked into Narka's
great blue-black eyes, and then opened her
arms.

Narka let herself sink into the loved embrace which had so long been her haven of
sweetest rest ; but suddenly she recollected
how that soft little hand had clutched an imaginary knout, to cut open the flesh of the

woman whom Basil loved. The recollection
made her blood run cold, and she drew
herself away from the clasping arms.

All this time a crowd of *gamins* were
collected at the door outside, staring at the
grand equipage and chaffing the fine flunky.
When the owner of this splendour came out,
they ceased their chaffing, and stood in
silence, watching the ceremony of her getting
into the carriage and sinking back on the
cushions, while the fine flunky arranged her
silken skirts, the glossy thoroughbreds meantime tossing their heads and pawing the
ground, and giving every sign of impatience
and disgust. Finally they moved on, spurn-
ing the stones contemptuously, and striking
sparks with their steel hoofs ; a comical
parody on human impudence and conceit
admirably performed by thoroughbred
beasts.

As the carriage with its liveries and em-
blazoned panels jolted lightly down the
roughly paved street, the pageant drew
gazers to doors and windows, and Sibyl

again passed under the fire of those sullen glances which to her betokened the excess of wickedness. Clearly these people needed to be held down with a hand of iron.

Narka watched the carriage out of sight from the doorstep. As she was turning in she saw Madame Blaquette standing in the middle of the street, and earnestly gazing into the palm of her hand.

'God direct me!' ejaculated the landlady, in a voice evidently intended to reach Narka. Then, looking up: 'Oh! it is you, mademoiselle! I was just considering whether I ought to bestow an alms on this poor woman or not; she *looks* deserving, but I *may* be deceived.'

'As you have taken out the penny, I think I would bestow it,' replied Narka.

'That is *precisely* what I feel about it. Then, in God's name, I will risk it!' She presented the penny to the beggar, who had been patiently waiting while her fate was discussed.

Narka glanced at her and noticed that she

wore green spectacles, and a bandage over one side of her surprisingly red face. 'I should not have said that she looked deserving,' was Narka's reflection as she turned indoors; 'but I don't suppose Madame Blaquette's penny will do her much harm.'

CHAPTER X.

RUMBLINGS OF THE STORM.

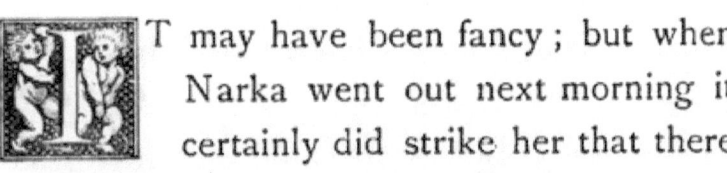T may have been fancy; but when Narka went out next morning it certainly did strike her that there was something abnormal in the looks of the people and the atmosphere of the place. But she set it down to the effect of Sibyl's shudderings and denunciations, and turned away from the idea. Moreover, her own nerves, she knew, were always at full stretch, generally beyond it, and it was always safe to discount her own impressions. She bethought her that she would go down to the House, and hear what they said there.

'Was Sibyl dreaming, or did she really smell brimstone in the air yesterday?' asked

Narka, walking into the dispensary, where
Marguerite was pounding herbs in a mortar.

'I'm afraid she smelt something,' Marguerite replied, without looking up. 'I wish
you had gone away with her.'

'I would not have gone if she had asked
me ; but she did not ask me.'

Marguerite made no comment on this, but
went on with her pounding.

'Oh, Marguerite, what a fool I have been
all my life !' Narka burst out passionately ;
'I see now Sibyl never cared a straw for me.
She never loved me a bit, and she has been
feeding me on false sacraments of love all my
life !'

'Mon dieu ! how you do exaggerate everything !' said Marguerite, looking up and
tossing her head ; 'you are so terribly
morbid that you turn everything in life to
tragedy.'

'And what has life been to me but a
tragedy ever since I can remember ? It is
easy for you to preach, but it is enough to
drive me mad to see how little Sibyl cares

about me! To hear her talking sentimental stuff about longing to hold my hand, when all this time she never asked how I managed not to starve! Good God! if I were in her place and she in mine! But I am a fool—a fool!' she repeated passionately.

'Yes,' said Marguerite, with uncivil acquiescence, while her cornette bobbed in merry accompaniment to the pestle; 'you were a fool when you made an idol of a creature; and, as I told you before, it is the tumbling down of your idol that is hurting you so terribly. You expect too much from Sibyl, because you gave her more than you ought to have given to any human creature.'

'Not near as much as you have given.'

'I?'

'Yes, you; you have given everything to human creatures: your time, your energies, your whole life. I never gave all that to Sibyl.'

The pestle stopped, and Marguerite looked up in amazement.

'But I have not given that to creatures? I have given it to God. That is just what makes the difference.'

There was no answer to this. It shifted the ground of the argument too far. After a moment's silence Narka said :

'And so you think there is going to be an *émeute?*'

'I am afraid there is something brewing. One feels the throbbing of the kettle before it boils over.' Marguerite laid her open hand downward on the air, as if touching water.

'Does it break out all in a moment like that?'

'So they tell me. Our Sisters have seen terrible explosions, just like gunpowder: the men go down into the streets and fight; barricades start up in every direction as if by magic, and then there is firing and slaughtering, and the seven devils are let loose and the people go mad; first their heads go mad, and then their hearts.'

'Do hearts go mad, Marguerite?'

'I think they must. I do believe that
hatred creates madness, just as fever does
when it gets to one's head. And it is so
much harder to cure a mad heart than a
mad head! Hatred is such a malignant
force! Where it breaks out it devours
everything; it is like fire. That is the
dreadful thing in these revolutions; they
are hatred in a state of combustion.'

'Are you afraid the people will attack the
House?'

'Oh no; they never hurt us. But a lot
of our poor people will get into sad trouble.
The police have been reinforced, and the
troops are consigned to the barracks, and
swarms of detectives are prowling about the
district. We have set the children to pray,
two by two, in the church all day, and M.
le Curé gave us leave to watch ourselves in
prayer all to-night.'

'Is it so near as all that?' Narka exclaimed, in surprise; 'and you never said a
word about it to me!'

'It was only this morning that we heard

how alarmed the Government was, and the stringent measures that are being taken.'

Marguerite put aside the pestle and mortar, and took down from the wall the little basket she carried on her errands.

'You are going to visit some sick people? Let me come with you,' said Narka.

'No; it is a case of small-pox; you had better go home. And if there be any movement in the streets to-morrow morning, stay indoors. It may blow off, as these threats sometimes do; or it may be held down. But we shall soon know. *Au revoir*, dear.'

They parted at the gate, and Narka went home. Now that her eyes had been opened to observe the signs of things that were coming, the rebellious element in the air had become distinctly sentient, and her pulses were quickened to sympathy with it. She too had wrongs to redress, and she was ready to side heart and soul with the people around her who were going to rebel and to seek redress for theirs. She did not stop to ask whether these wrongs were real or not;

she was in a mood to applaud rebellion ; her whole heart went out in sympathy with it. These people, like her, were the victims of tyranny ; they were politically free, but they were the slaves of those merciless tyrants, the rich ; they were starved and exasperated to violence by the inexorable rapacity of the capitalists. This might be justice in the eyes of the law, but in the sight of God it was murder. In the sight of God the rich man had no more right to use the brute force of money against the poor one than the strong man to use the brute force of muscular strength against the helpless paralytic. But they arrogated the right, and this was the universal wrong that was crying out for vengeance all over the world.

The passion of revenge had been sleeping in Narka's heart, ready to wake up at the first opportunity. Time had not made less heinous in her eyes any of the wrongs that she had suffered, or weakened her sense of their injustice. Herein lies the vital difference between pain and evil : the flight of

time, passing over pain, effaces the very
remembrance of it, and washes away the
traces of suffering; but it leaves the memory
of evil and the ruin it has made untouched;
the lapse of years atones for nothing; forget-
fulness is not remedial of guilt. It was not the
fact of her father and brother having died in
Siberia, of her mother lying in the graveyard at Yrakow—it was not these sorrows in
themselves that rankled and festered in
Narka's heart, making it burn for revenge
and throb in passionate sympathy with rebellion; it was the fact that those deaths
were the work of human cruelty and injustice. What could be done to better the
world while these sinister powers of evil were
ruling it? There was nothing but to rise up
and destroy them.

She got out those articles of Basil's and
read them. They were like the sound of
martial music to her excited nerves. She
was putting them away, when the concierge
knocked at her door, and handed in a letter.
It was from Ivan. Was this news of Basil?

Narka opened it eagerly. This is what Ivan said :

'On the 10th, there will be a meeting at which some important news will be communicated. If you don't write to forbid me, I will meet you in the gallery of the Luxembourg on Friday at half-past one, and we will go together.'

This invitation would have been to Narka like the braying of the trumpet to the warhorse, if she had not already been to one of the assemblies in question. She suspected the news was about Basil, but even this temptation could not lure her again into the company of Olga Borzidoff and the rest of them.

She was ready to sympathize actively in every effort to overthrow tyrants ; but she would rather go out and fight on the barricades, if barricades there were to be, than deliberately come into contact with the people she had met before at these clandestine meetings. Besides, who could tell what might happen between this and the 10th ?

She went to bed late, and dreamed all night of Basil, of dangers shared with him, of hair-breadth escapes, of rescue at last, and then she awoke and found herself still alone, and life still a tragedy in which the romance of love had yet to be enacted.

CHAPTER XI.

LA VILLETTE IN ARMS.

WHEN Narka went out to make her little provisions next morning, she perceived at once that there was a movement of some sort on foot. The people were out in the streets talking excitedly in groups. She asked a young workman what was the matter.

'The people have risen!' he said triumphantly; 'I have been helping at the barricades since daybreak; I have only run off to get a mouthful of food. We are going to have a *journée!* Keep indoors, *ma belle citoyenne*—the troops are coming down the boulevards—unless you like to come and lend us a hand on the barricades?'

He marched off in high good-humour, proud as a peacock ; the women were looking after him, some like furies, others scared and anxious.

Narka hurried home, made a hasty meal, and put on her bonnet to go down to the House. As she opened her own door she saw Dr. Schenk on the threshold, with his hand on the bell.

'You are going out !' he said, in surprise.

'Yes ; I am going to the Sisters' House. It seems there is an *émeute.*'

She stood back, and he came in.

'Yes, a very serious *émeute.* You must not venture out into the streets ; the firing may begin anywhere at any moment. I have come to take you away. You can't remain here in the midst of such danger. Put up what you want in a little bag, and come away at once. I have a cab waiting at the corner of the Rue X—— ; we can get round through a back way.'

He spoke with quiet authority, just as when she had been his patient he had

ordered her to do this, or avoid that. Narka
was bewildered.

'Where do you want to take me to?' she
said.

Dr. Schenk looked at her in silence with a
steady gaze that had something magnetic in
it. Then, drawing a step nearer:

'There is only one place where you can go
with safety and dignity,' he said; 'that is
your husband's house. Don't start, Narka;
listen to me. I have loved you from the
first hour we met. I did not dare to tell you
so, because I was afraid it might have driven
you from me. I knew you must be slowly
won, and I was satisfied to wait. I would
have waited seven years. But there is no
time to wait now; I am driven to speak; it
is the only way of rescuing you. I love you!
Accept me for your husband, and I will trust
to winning your love by the strength of my
own, by the whole devotion of my life.'

Narka had been too startled and surprised
to speak.

'Why, I thought you knew,' she said,

hesitating, and her colour rose and spread to a beautiful carmine. 'Did not Ivan tell you? I am engaged to Basil Zorokoff.'

'That is an idle dream,' said Schenk, unmoved. 'You will never be Zorokoff's wife.'

'What do you mean?'

'He will never marry you; he does not love you.'

'How dare you say that!' cried Narka, and the blue fire flashed from her eyes.

'He does not love you,' Schenk repeated, in the same quiet tone. 'If he loved you, he would not have left you all this time to work for your daily bread alone, battling with the perils and cruelties of want. Don't tell me he could not help it. If he had loved you he would have helped it; but he loves nothing but ambition. He might have married you, from a sense of honour, if he had been his own master. But love you! Child, your love sweeps over him in a high tide of passion that he no more vibrates to than an oyster vibrates to the roll of the Atlantic!'

The words were full of passion, but Schenk's voice was as cold and level as if he had been speaking on any ordinary subject ; the fire in him was at white heat ; but it did not flash out ; it was concentrated within. There was something unhuman in this cold-blooded self-command that repelled Narka indescribably ; but it helped her to be calm.

'Dr. Schenk,' she said, trying to keep her loathing out of her voice. 'I will not forget that you have shown me great kindness ; but I must remind you that nothing can justify your speaking of what is strictly and sacredly personal to me. I am as sure of the love of Basil Zorokoff as I am of mine for him. You are not capable of understanding a nature like his. He is too far above you.'

Schenk smiled compassionately.

'Keep your illusions,' he said ; 'I don't wan't to destroy them ; I only want to prevent them from destroying you. You are sacrificing your youth to a phantom. Zorokoff will never break through his present bonds to marry you. His own indifference is

in league with the strong will of his father
and his sister. Give up that dream. Worship him as a patriot, if you will, but give
your love to me. I love you with my whole
soul ; I will be your slave all my life. You
care nothing for the gauds that other women
covet ; but these, too, I can put at your feet ;
my fortune is ample. Be my wife, Narka,
and let us work in the good cause together !'
He held out his hand to her, but she fell
back with a gesture of denial. Schenk
thought it expressed disgust. ' My hand
is clean ; there is no man's blood upon it,'
he said, and there was a sinister gleam in his
eye.

Narka, stung to the quick, flashed back at
him a glance of hatred and defiance.

' That taunt covers a cowardly lie !' she
said ; ' but I am glad that you uttered it ; it
shows me your true character, and enables
me to dismiss you without a shadow of regret.
Go, and never cross my path again !'

She pointed to the door, but Schenk did
not obey her. He turned away, and paced

the room twice—three times; his head was
bent, his right hand was thrust into his
breast, his features were working convul-
sively. There was something terrible and
pitiable in the sight of this sudden passion,
in the agony of conflict that was going on
within him. Narka, standing by the mantelpiece, watched him, divided between fear,
anger, and a rising sense of pity. He had
flung his love so generously at her feet, she
felt sorry for him, in spite of those insolent
and cruel words.

Suddenly Schenk came and stood before
her. The change that had taken place in
him within the last few minutes was frightful
to see; his sallow pallor had turned to a livid
gray; there was a red line across his forehead, as if he had been struck with a lash.

'Forgive me,' he said meekly; 'I have
behaved like a fool and a brute. My love
for you must be my excuse. I love you so
madly there is nothing under heaven I would
not have done to win you! But I will never
trouble you again. Try and forgive what I

said of Zorokoff. There was nothing in it. It was the fling of a jealous man. Jealousy makes men mad. I was mad just now. But it is past. And now what can I do to help you? Is there no friend that you can go to?'

Narka's passionate anger was disarmed, but with it her strength of self-command gave way. She struggled to hold it for a moment, and then burst into tears. Schenk forced her gently into a seat, and stood over her, waiting.

'I am very sorry this has happened,' she said, after a while, lifting her head and swallowing a sob; 'I am very sorry. No; there is nothing you can do for me. Good-bye.'

'I can't bear the idea of your being here alone,' he said. 'Is there no one within reach?—Madame de Beaucrillon?'

Narka made a negative movement with her head.

'I don't run the risks up here that you imagine. The people won't hurt me. I am

Sœur Marguerite's friend. I was going down
to the House to see her.'

She stood up. Schenk saw there was no
use in urging her.

'I will see you that far,' he said; 'as yet
the road there is clear.'

He opened the door, and they went out
together.

Narka noticed the beggar standing at the
door of the house opposite. It struck her as
odd that she should be quietly stationed there
waiting for pennies at such a crisis, for nobody
was abroad except those who were going to
fight. The street had already undergone a
change : every shop that had a shutter had
put it up, and everybody had gone indoors.

Narka saw and felt the change without
being conscious of it. Those cruel words of
Schenk's, ' He might marry you from a sense
of honour, but he does not love you,' were
like the bite of a snake in her flesh. They
walked on rapidly to the House, and did not
speak until Schenk said good-bye to her at
the gate.

The court was a scene of extraordinary excitement ; people were coming and going ; the children of the schools were flocking in ; they had been sent home, but the parents had come back with them, entreating the Sisters to keep them over the night.

' But where are we to put them ?' exclaimed Sœur Jeanne, in dismay ; ' every bed, every mattress in the house is more than filled !'

' Pack them up to the infirmary,' suggested Marguerite.

' The infirmary !' retorted Sœur Jeanne, ' there are ninety children packed into it already ; they have hardly room to turn round.'

' What does that matter, *ma sœur ?*' urged Marguerite ; ' where there is no room for ninety, there is room enough for a hundred. Get along with you all to the infirmary !'

And the children, in high glee at the lawless opportunity, went tumbling up the stairs.

' Oh, Narka, I am so thankful to see you !' cried Marguerite, perceiving her. ' Here is a note from Sibyl ; it has just come. She wants us both to go off with her to Beau-crillon by the noon express.'

'Are you going?' inquired Narka.

'I? What a notion! I thought nobody but Sibyl could have imagined such a thing possible. Just think how busy we are going to be! The big school-room is turned into an ambulance, and they will be carrying in the wounded as soon as the fighting begins.'

While she spoke there was a detonation of fire-arms, first a single shot, then a volley, followed by a prolonged shout that rose in the distance, and came gradually nearer as street after street took it up. The women who were in the court hurried away; the Sisters went quickly indoors with the children, who had lingered outside, full of curiosity and delighted excitement. In the twinkling of an eye the place was cleared, and Marguerite and Narka were left alone at the gate.

'You had better run home at once,' said Marguerite; 'the road is still clear. But don't loiter, and don't stir out while the firing lasts. It is not likely——'

The sentence was cut short by a terrific volley that sounded much nearer this time. Marguerite turned pale, and made the sign of the cross.

'Why may I not stay here with you?' said Narka.   'I could help in the ambulance?'

'Yes, you might,'—Marguerite hesitated— 'only I may be sent down to the barricades to attend to the wounded who can't be carried here.   Still, if you like——'

As she spoke, there came rushing past the gate a band of roughs, shouldering muskets and shouting a ribald song.

'And these are the people you are going to risk your life for?' said Narka; 'men who probably don't even know the name of God!'

'Perhaps not; but God knows their name, and has died for every one of them.   That is why it is worth while,' replied Marguerite.

She spoke calmly, but Narka could see that she was agitated.

'Are you not afraid, dear?' she said, looking tenderly down on the small figure.

'Afraid?'   The question implied some-

thing which stirred Marguerite's blood.
Noli irritare leonem was the motto of her
house, and though the lion lay dormant
beneath the dove, just as the lady's silken
attire had disappeared under the peasant's
gown, there were moments when the lion
woke up, and when the antique French patri-
cian, than whom the womanhood of all the
races offers no loftier or lovelier type, asserted
her inalienable dignity ; 'no, I am not afraid,'
she said, with penitent humility ; 'what is
there to be afraid of ?'

'The firing, the bullets : suppose you were
to be killed ?'

'Killed ? No such luck !' Marguerite
shook her head.

A suspicion darted through Narka's mind.

'Marguerite, you are wearied of your life.'
she said.

'Wearied of my life ? I should never be
wearied of it if I did not get homesick now
and then.'

'Ah! Then you do regret the life you
have renounced ?'

Marguerite looked up in quick surprise and laughed.

'I meant homesick for heaven. If I were shot down at the barricades in the service of charity, it would be like martyrdom, and I should go straight to heaven. Would not that be luck, dear Narka? Only such a grand death is much too good for me to expect.'

She gave a little sigh. She looked very tired, though she was excited. Something in her manner and voice struck Narka to the heart. Could it be that this longing for martyrdom was prophetic? Narka resolved to stay and share the risks, whatever they might be.

CHAPTER XII.

NARKA'S LULLABY.

THE *émeute* lasted six days. Then came peace and the day of reckoning, while La Viilette cowered in its kennel like a whipped hound. Numbers who had been taken fighting on the barricades and in the streets were in prison ; but greater numbers still had escaped, and amongst them many of the ringleaders, and these were skulking in holes and corners, nursing their wounds, and dodging the police who were in hot pursuit of them.

The white cornettes had been the confidantes of the people all through. Every day, before dawn, wives and mothers were to be seen waiting at the gate of the House, asking for help and shelter for husbands and sons and brothers : 'mon homme' had held a barricade for ten hours, and was a dead man if the police caught him ; and so on with scores of others.

Marguerite's wish had been disappointed. She had been a martyr only in spirit and in self-sacrifice ; but, in the eyes of the people, she had won the palm-branch as fully as if she had shed her blood for them. They had loved her before—they now worshipped her ; and Narka, who had been her companion through those terrible days, shared the prestige that surrounded her. Early on the morning of the seventh day they went out together on their stealthy round of iliegal visits of mercy through the district; and it was a fresh wonder to Narka to see how Marguerite rose to the new and strange difficulties of the position. Sometimes she spoke to the culprits in a tone of severe command, so amusingly at variance with her little figure and her sweet young face that it raised a smile; but this unconscious air of comedy in no way detracted from the impressiveness of what she said. To those who were expiating their criminal folly in bodily pain, suffering from wounds and from remorse, her compassion was boundless; her voice was full of pity and healing balm, and her smile had a pathos that is seen only on lips that have quivered with pain. As Narka went with her through the reeking slums and tenements, and saw her exorcising the evil spirits, subduing impotent rage to humble penitence, making the haters ashamed of their hate, her own passionate theories for reforming the world suddenly appeared to her, not merely futile, but insane and cruel beside this simple philosophy of love.

They came presently to the door of Antoine Drex's house. Antoine was hiding. He had been recklessly prominent all through the riots, and the police were actively searching for him. The Sisters brought him food secretly, and Marguerite came regularly to dress his wounds. He had left his own

lodging, and taken refuge with his old mother
in this miserable tenement, recently inhabited
by a man who had fallen on a barricade, and
whose idiot child was now moaning on its
bed with fever, while la mère Drex tried to
soothe it.

Narka assisted Marguerite in dressing the
wound ; it was a bad one in the head, but
not dangerous.   When this was done she
went to see if the child wanted any help.

'Santez ! santez !' wailed the little creature,
staring at her with mindless eyes, now glittering with the light of fever.

'What is she calling for ?' Narka asked.

'She wants me to sing to her,' said the
old woman.   'Poor Binard used to sing the
child to sleep of a night ; a good thing it was
for him too—it kept him from the cabaret
ever since his wife's death.   I can't, *ma
petiote*, I can't,' she repeated, as the child
kept on her monotonous cry :

'Santez ! santez !'

In the excitement and busy exertions of
the last week, Narka had almost forgotten

her lost voice ; but this piteous supplication of the sick child reminded her of it, and smote her with a new regret. With a sudden intense desire, there came to her a vivifying inward force, swift and potent as the touch of an electric spring. She cleared her throat and began to warble, first in a soft undertone, as if trying an instrument that she was not sure of—whose strings might snap ; but gradually her voice rose, and gained in volume, and rang out in the old clear, sweet tones.

Marguerite could hardly believe her ears. It seemed like a miracle : one of those miracles of charity that she herself performed day after day in the desolate places. She crushed the sugar noiselessly in the tisane she was preparing for Antoine Drex, and kept murmuring to herself, with a smile :

'God is love ! God is love !'

Antoine's eyes were fixed on Narka as if she were some visitant from another world. She looked like one, as she sat singing by the poverty-stricken bed, the flush of a pure emotion on her face, a light of joy in her luminous dark eyes.

When the song—a Russian ballad—was ended, the child called out :

' Enco' ! enco' !'

And Narka, stirred by that encore as she had never been by the applause of a salon, sang again, this time in French, Mignon's lament, ' Rendez-moi la patrie, ou laissez-moi mourir !'

The child grew calmer, and ceased to toss on her pillow ; by the time the song was ended she had fallen asleep. La mère Drex lifted up her hands in a gesture of wonderment and admiration.

Narka rose, and moved softly out of the room after Marguerite. When they were on the landing, by a common impulse the two friends turned and kissed one another. Their hearts were too full for speech.

On reaching the bottom of the stairs they found a crowd assembled before the house. Marguerite at once guessed that the police had tracked Antoine, and stepped bravely forward to meet the enemy.

'What is the matter?' she said.

'Ma sœur,' answered a *blouse*, 'we wanted to see whether it was you or the Virgin Mary that was singing up there.'

'It was neither one nor the other, you silly people!' said Marguerite, intensely relieved; 'it was my friend'— pointing to Narka. 'Hush!' she cried, seeing they were going to cheer; 'there is a sick child up there that has just fallen asleep. Don't wake her!'

Obedient to Sœur Marguerite, as usual, they walked on silently, making an escort to her and Narka across the court, and accompanying them to the end of the lane beyond it. Then, as by a common accord, they raised a ringing cheer:

'Vive le rossignol! Vive l'amie de la Sœur Marguerite!'

The ovation brought the wild roses into Narka's cheeks, and made her heart swell with a sense of victory unlike anything she had ever felt before.

It had been an exciting morning, and she

was very tired as she walked home. On
reaching her own door it suddenly occurred
to her that this was the tenth, the day of the
meeting. At this very hour it was in full
swing, and Ivan Gorff was probably wondering why she had neither written nor met him
at the trysting-place.

CHAPTER XIII.

MARGUERITE DISOBEYS THE LAW.

UST as Narka had shut herself in and sat down to realize the happy fact of her voice's return, the main street of the Place was thrown into excitement by an accident. A cab containing two men was coming quietly up the street, when the horse took fright and rushed blindly on, struck against a cart, and fell, overturning the cab. One of the travellers, who was in the act of jumping out, paid for his want of presence of mind by an ugly cut in the head; the other, in attempting to follow him, had hurt his leg, and lay groaning in the bottom of the overturned cab.

Two *gamins* jumped up on the wheel to look in at him.

' It is the Commissary of Police !' cried one of them, turning to the bystanders.

His face was a picture ; it expressed a keen sense of the humorous side of the situation, with a dread of 'catching it ' if he were overheard by the still powerful, though prostrate, functionary. For it was, in truth, no less a person than the mighty Commissary who lay trapped in the upset vehicle, groaning with a sprained ankle, like a common man.

A crowd had gathered in a moment. No one recognised the man on the pavement, but all shrewdly suspected him to be a police agent, come to participate in some important arrest. Anyhow, the pair were after no good. It was clearly a judgment of Providence that had overtaken them, in favour of the poor wretch they were after, and the fun of the thing was delicious. People came, nevertheless, from the neighbouring shops and volunteered help, and the cab was soon set on its wheels.

' I have hurt my foot badly,' said the Commissary. 'Is there a doctor anywhere near?'

'We are close to the Sisters' House, monsieur,' said a workman; 'you had better let us take you there while the doctor is fetched.'

Another cab was called, and the two injured men were helped into it and driven off.

Sœur Marguerite was in the dispensary, and saw it stop at the gate with a procession of ragamuffins. Presently the two Commissaries were assisted across the court into the House. In a moment several Sisters were in attendance. The injuries proved more painful than serious, and the Sisters were quite capable of dealing with them without the doctor.

As soon as the Commissary's sprain had been attended to, and he was made comfortable on an improvised sofa, with pillows at his back, he asked for writing materials, and wrote a short note. Then, beckoning to Marguerite:

' Ma sœur,' he said, in a confidential tone, ' I want you to do a little commission for me.

I want you to take a cab and drive to the Préfecture, and ask to see M. le Préfet—you will send in my card—and then give this note into his hands.'

' Ah !'

Marguerite's look of intense curiosity as she took the note was irresistible.

' I will tell you what it is about,' whispered the Commissary. ' I and my colleague came here to arrest a scoundrel named Drex— Antoine Drex ; but we have been hindered, as you see. Now, it is most necessary that they should know this at once at the Préfecture, and send on two others to do it, or the fellow may get wind of the matter and slip through our fingers. You understand ?'

' Oh yes, monsieur, I understand.' Marguerite's heart was thumping so that she wondered the Commissary did not hear it and suspect. ' I don't think they would let me see M. le Préfet,' she said, turning the letter in her hand ; ' had I not better say you want some one to be sent up here to you ?'

' No, no ; that would lose too much time,'

he said impatiently. 'They will let you in at once when you show my card with that word written on it.'

'Is he suspected of anything very bad, this Antoine Drex?' she inquired, with an idea that every minute's delay might help Antoine.

'He is not suspected, he is known to be a dangerous villain. Go, ma sœur; not a word to anyone here, but go!'

Marguerite slipped the letter up her sleeve, and went out. Once in the street, she stood debating. It was a hard task that was set her. Must she execute it? Poor Antoine! She knew he was more sinned against than sinning. Still a voice whispered, '*You are bound to obey the law.*' She heard it; still she hesitated. Suddenly another voice whispered, 'Charity is the greatest commandment of all. *Charity is the law of God.*' She agreed with this voice; still she hesitated, but not long. Glancing quickly, furtively, up and down the street, she started off in the direction of the Cour des Chats, walking as fast as she dared, and quickening

her pace to a run when she turned into the
dirty laneway that led into it.

Antoine was sitting as she had left him,
only smoking a pipe. His mother had gone
out to the *lavoir;* the idiot child, lulled to
rest by Narka's song, was still fast asleep.

Marguerite closed the door, and then,
dropping her voice :

'Antoine,' she said, ' the police are in
pursuit of you. The Commissary was on his
way here when he met with an accident ; he
is now at the House, resting, and I am going
to the Préfecture with this letter, desiring
some one to be sent to arrest you.'

Without waiting to see the effect of her
information, she turned quickly away, and
closed the door after her.

An hour later two police-officers drove
up to the entrance of the Cour des Chats,
and crossed over to the house where Antoine
was lodging. They went up and knocked at
the door, guided by the instructions contained
in the Commissary's letter. Some one said,
' Come in '; but on opening the door they

beheld, instead of Antoine Drex, Sœur Marguerite, knitting by the window.

'Pardon, ma sœur,' said one of the agents,
taking off his hat; 'we are looking for
Antoine Drex. We have come to arrest
him.'

Marguerite's heart was beating like a
hammer on an anvil, but she looked at him,
and said composedly:

'You had better go to the House, and tell
M. le Commissaire that you found me here
in place of Antoine Drex.'

The two police-officers looked at her as if
they doubted her sanity. Presently they
began to understand. They were young,
they were brave, they had hearts of men.

'Ma sœur, I have the honour to salute
you,' said one of them.

They both bowed and walked out of the
room, and Marguerite heard the sound of
smothered laughter on the stairs.

But there remained now the Commissary
to face. She knew there would be no sympathetic laughter there. The Commissary,

indeed, flew into a great rage when he heard
the trick that had been played him ; he sent
for the Superior, and whipped Marguerite on
her unoffending back ; he threatened to denounce the community as accomplices of all
the rebels and rascals of the district, to have
the House shut up, etc., etc.

Marguerite meantime had followed the
agents to the House, and walked bravely in to
receive her reward. She was very frightened,
but she did not show it, and this assumption
of coolness made matters worse.

‘ So, ma sœur, this is how you respect the
law !’ cried the angry Commissary ; ‘ before
you went to the Préfecture you gave that
scoundrel a hint to skedaddle.’

‘ Monsieur le Commissaire, I am incapable
of anything so mean,’ replied Marguerite ; ‘ I
told him plainly that I was going to the Préfecture with a message from you for his arrest.’

‘ And you are not ashamed of helping a
blackguard like that to evade the law ?’

‘ Antoine Drex is not a blackguard, Monsieur le Commissaire ; he is an honest man ;

he has been very unhappy ; he was cruelly
and unjustly treated, and he is exasperated.
He was falsely accused of murdering his
drunken wife, and kept ten months in prison
with thieves and homicides before he was put
on his trial and acquitted. He came out of
prison with his health broken and his heart
maddened, and he has never got back into his
right heart since. The injustice and cruelty
of the law turned him into a rebel. And so
it would have done you or me, M. le Commissaire.'

'I'll tell you what,' said the Commissary,
'I will report you to the Minister as a rebel
more dangerous than a score of Antoine
Drexes.'

He was furious ; but as he vented his fury,
something in her young face, an expression
at once timid and dauntless, reproachful and
beseeching, went to his heart. He turned
away with an angry grunt, and remained
silent ; while Marguerite picked up and re-
placed at his back the pillow that, in his
agitation, he had sent rolling to the floor.

A cab was now waiting to take him and his colleague away. Before he left, he spoke civilly to Sœur Jeanne, and told her to look after Sœur Marguerite, and see that she played no tricks with the law in future, for she might fall next time on some one who would be less ready to overlook her misdemeanours.

Sœur Jeanne scolded Marguerite; but the community had a merry time of it at recreation that evening; nor were they to be checked in their fun over the Commissary's misadventure and the sorry figure he made in his official discomfiture by Sœur Jeanne's attempt to frown and look aggrieved.

Narka had heard nothing of the event, not having left home since she had parted from Marguerite. At ten o'clock that night she was a little startled by some one knocking at her door. She supposed it was the concierge with a letter; but before opening she asked who was there.

A voice that she did not recognise answered

' A friend of Sœur Marguerite.'

Narka drew back the bolt. She did not know what fear was, but she was conscious of an unpleasant sensation when she beheld a huge man, with his head and shoulders concealed by a shawl, step quickly in and close the door behind him. He threw back the shawl, and Narka recognised Antoine Drex. He told her what had happened, and how he had been hidden in a wood-yard all the afternoon and evening, and now implored her to shelter him till morning, and give him some food. She fetched him bread and wine and some cold meat, and he rolled an arm-chair into the little kitchen, which was the only *annexe* to the salon-bedroom. But Antoine declared he was lodged like a préfet.

Narka was glad to harbour a hunted fellow-creature, to give sanctuary to a victim of that long-armed, cruel tyrant, the law. Very likely Antoine was deep-dyed in plots against the Government ; but Narka was not the one to think worse of any man for that. Every political criminal was dear to her for Basil's sake. Nevertheless, though she was glad to open her door to Drex, she felt that in doing so she was incurring a great personal risk, and if Antoine rested easily, she did not. All night long she lay awake, listening to every sound ; a dog that barked, a cart that rumbled, made her start. She was up before Antoine gave signs of stirring. She prepared some food for him, and when he had partaken of it, he stole out in the early morn, his shawl drawn round him, and went down to the House just as the gate was opened.

CHAPTER XIV.

NARKA SINGS FOR JOY.

NARKA never gave a thought to the possible consequences to herself, from the moment she saw Antoine Drex safe out of her house; but the event had excited her extraordinarily. She forgot that his coming to her for shelter was the natural enough result of her visit to him with Marguerite in the morning, and she magnified the incident into a portent. Surely she must be destined to play some part in this great revolutionary drama that was being enacted all over Europe, or else why did these chances pursue her? Some event was at hand, she said to herself, some great

event, in which a *rôle* was reserved to her by
fate, or by Providence.

'Do you believe in presentiments?' she
asked Marguerite, when they met that afternoon.

'Certainly!' was the emphatic rejoinder;
'I believe them to be a sign of indigestion.'

Marguerite knew that Narka was morbidly
fanciful at times, and she made a point of
snubbing her fancies. Just now she seemed
exaltée and overwrought.

Nothing occurred during the day to justify
her presentiments, but at about ten o'clock
that night she was again startled by a visitor.
This time it was a ring, a very light ring, but
to her imagination, on the watch for signs
and portents, it sounded preternaturally loud
in the stillness. Could it be Antoine come
back? Marguerite had said they would
shelter him at the House until he could get
away to Calvados, his native place. Narka
went to the door and asked who was there.

A voice answered in Russian, 'It is I,
Narka.'

Her heart gave a great leap, a low cry rose to her lips, the bolt flew back—she never knew how—and she found herself in Basil Zorokoff's arms. For one long moment life seemed over ; she was conscious of nothing but the wild rapture of that embrace; his strong arms were clasping her, his cheek was pressed against hers. Was it some sweet madness, or was she in heaven ?

'Are we alone ?' he whispered, glancing round the dimly lighted room, while he relaxed his hold of her.

' Yes, quite alone. Oh, Basil, is it you, or am I dreaming ?'

She trembled and clung to him as if she were afraid he would escape from her. Basil drew her to the little couch, and they sat down together.

' I frightened you,' he said, laughing ; ' I ought to have given you warning, and not come down on you like this ; but there was no time, unless I telegraphed on the road, and that would have been a risk.'

' I am not a bit frightened, only beside

myself with joy. Oh, Basil! Basil! my love! my love!'

She looked up into his face, sobbing for happiness.

He bent down and kissed her tenderly. She could see that he was aged; but also that he was grander and handsomer than ever.

'Where have you come from?' she said; 'have you escaped, or did the Prince consent to your coming away?'

'Consent?' Basil threw back his head with the gesture she remembered so well: 'I escaped in disguise by the same train that took him to Berlin in attendance on the Emperor, who is gone to visit his brother Kaiser.'

'Then he does not know that you have escaped?'

'He knows it by this time, and he is tearing his hair and swearing by St. Nicholas that Basil Zorokoff is the greatest wretch under heaven. Oh! it is a fine thing to be a loyal subject, and hate one's own flesh and blood for love of the Emperor!'

'When did you get here?' asked Narka.

'An hour ago. I have come on here from the train.'

'Then you have not seen Sibyl? You did not know she is in town?'

'I did know; but I came straight to you.'

'My own, my own. . . .' She locked her arms round his throat, and let her head drop on his breast. 'You came first to me!'

'Of course I came first to you. Let me look at you.' He put his hand under her chin, and held up her face so that the light from the shaded lamp fell upon it. 'My poor Narka,' he said, gazing at her with great tenderness, and then kissing her, 'you are grown thinner; but you are as beautiful as ever. And in spite of all you have gone through—the prison——'

He felt her shudder in his arms, and she nestled closer to him.

'Don't let us talk of that,' she said, in a low voice; 'it is all past, and we are together. I want to hear about you. Tell me everything ; tell me all that has happened since we parted. Remember how little I know : only first hints from Sibyl in her letters, and since then, stray news of you through Ivan Gorff. Tell me the story yourself now.'

And Basil, with his arm round her, and her hands locked about his neck, told it rapidly, passing lightly over all that was too painful and humiliating, so as not to lacerate her loving heart, but enlarging complacently on the work he had done, the results he had achieved, the brilliant hopes he cherished.

Narka saw with pride that he had ripened greatly during the interval of their separation ; his mind had gained in shrewdness and insight, his faculties had evidently grown in power of concentration ; she was amazed at the vigour and quickness with which he summed up the situation, weighed chances, forecast probabilities, and arrived at practical conclusions. It was clear that he had thrown his whole soul and his whole energies into the service of patriotism. He looked a

patriot and a hero every inch, so strong and
straight and bold in his manly beauty ; a
lover for a queen to be proud of. And
Narka was proud of him ; her heart swelled
with pride in him ; she admired him more
than ever, and she loved him with her whole
soul. And yet—she was conscious of a disappointment somewhere. It was noble in
him to be absorbed in this grand impersonal
object, to have cast away, for the sake of
serving his oppressed fellow-countrymen, all
the pleasure that his youth and rank might
have claimed ; she admired and applauded
the nobleness that this choice evinced, and
yet — there was a vague disappointment
somewhere. Schenk's cruel words recurred
to her with a sting that even the joy of
Basil's presence could not allay : '*He does
not love you ; he only loves his ambition. If
he marries you, it will be from a sense of
honour.*' Yet Basil was her affianced lover ;
and she was beautiful ; and he had come to
her before he went to the sister whom he
loved so dearly. How could she doubt

but that he loved her? If only he had
lingered a little longer on the joy of their
meeting, and then entered eagerly on the
question of their approaching marriage!

'And Sibyl?' he said; 'she has been true
to you?'

'In what sense true? Does she know of
our engagement?'

'I took it for granted she did.'

'She never let me suspect it if she did.
And, dear Basil, I am afraid she will resent
our marriage as bitterly as the Prince.'

'I hope not, when she knows the whole
truth—when I tell her how dear you are to
me, and how much I owe you. I hope to
win her consent without great difficulty. She
will be so glad to see me, it will be easier to
persuade her.'

Narka's heart sank a little. Was Sibyl's
consent, then, essential?

'You see,' Basil went on, 'we are still in
my father's power. I am absolutely penniless
if he does not relent, and I could not ask
you to marry a beggar. I have brought

trouble enough already on you, God knows, without that.'

'Oh, but I am going to make our fortune,' Narka said, with a sudden thrill of exultation. And she told him of Zampa's offer, and the splendid career that was ready waiting for her.

'And I am to live in idleness while you work?' Basil said with a laugh; and he caressed her.

'You will be working for the great cause, while I work for bread. Don't you love me well enough to eat my bread?' She drew herself up, and keeping one hand round his neck, she laid the other upon his breast. 'Say, Basil, do you not love me well enough to eat my bread?'

He took her hand and kissed it, and held it clasped. 'The husband ought to work for the wife,' he said, 'not the wife for the husband.'

'That is the philosophy of pride and of your aristocratic traditions. A patriot should be above such prejudice. Marguerite was glad when she heard this chance of helping you was in store for me.'

'Marguerite! Ah! how is she?' There was a tender cadence in his voice as he said the name; it struck cold on Narka's heart.

'She is very well. I see her every day.'

'Does she seem happy?'

'She is happy, perfectly happy. She loves her vocation.'

'Ah! That vocation is a wonderful thing. But she was an angel always, Marguerite.'

Nobody knew this better than Narka, yet to hear Basil say it, and pronounce Marguerite's name in that soft undertone, burned her like the sting of a wasp.

'Good heavens! is that midnight?' he exclaimed, as the little clock on the mantelpiece struck the hour. 'How the time has sped! I have kept you up so late, dearest; and I have not slept myself for four nights.'

He made a movement to rise, but Narka clung and nestled to him.

'Must you go?' she said, rubbing her cheek against his coat caressingly. 'Tell me about Sibyl; will she be very angry with you for coming to me first ?'

'I don't mean to tell her. I shan't say I have seen you.'

'Ah! Yet it might be a good way of breaking the truth to her.'

'I could not begin by vexing her and making her jealous. She has been the best of sisters to me always. No one has ever loved me better than Sibyl, except you, Narka.'

The words were sweet, and tenderly spoken; but he might have pressed her to his heart, Narka thought, for his arm was round her. The next moment she mocked at herself for this ingenuity of self-torture. He had flown to her first; he had proved by this that she was his chief, his first object. Why could not she rest on that and be content, and silence these promptings of sick jealousy ? It was natural as well as generous and unselfish in him to consider Sibyl, and Narka admired the large-hearted love that embraced every claim so faithfully.

'When shall I see you again, darling?' she said, as he gently unwound her arms and stood up.

'I will come as early as I can to-morrow,' he replied, 'unless Sibyl sends for you to come and meet me at her house.'

'Oh no, not that!' said Narka, shrinking; 'I could not go through the comedy of a first meeting before Sibyl!'

'Then I will come here and fetch you, and we will go back to her together.'

She went out with him to the dark entry. At the outer door he turned once more and folded her in a close embrace. As he released her he whispered:

'When you see Marguerite you may tell her I am here. She will be glad to know that I am safe.'

'Yes, I will tell her,' Narka replied.

It was kind and natural that he should think of sending a message to Marguerite.

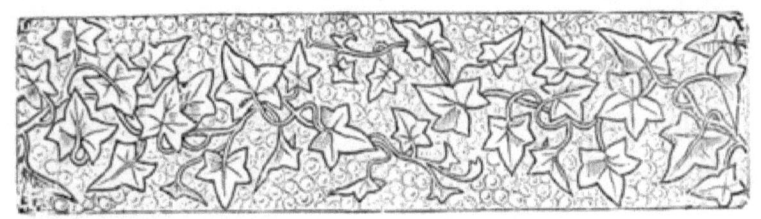

CHAPTER XV.

'IN THE NAME OF THE EMPEROR.'

NARKA was up before the earliest bell. When she looked round her it seemed wonderful that nothing was changed in the shabby room; that last night's vision had not left some visible trail of light or beauty behind it.

'My love! my love! did I dream that you were here, that you held me in your arms and kissed me? My Basil! my own!'

She struck her hands together, and laughed out loud for joy. The little morning duties were quickly performed, the frugal meal made ready and partaken of; then she dressed herself with care, inspired by the coquetry of love, and made the room as pretty as she could, arranging the flowers she had bought of a poor woman at the door, placing the books to the best advantage on the table, moving and changing everything, as if the magic of love's touch must improve the homely furniture. Then she sat down to the piano, and began to warble and trill with the full-throated rapture of a thrush in spring. She fancied Basil listening to her; she fancied herself bringing down La Scala in thunders of applause, and gathering up gold in bushels and pouring it out at his feet; she saw herself ministering to his wants, making his home bright and beautiful, and setting him free to work with a liberated mind in the great cause he had espoused. Suddenly, in the midst of these dreams, she remembered that her music might drown the sound of his ring, so she came away from the piano and moved about, changing the chairs and the books again, and smiling at everything, and humming for very inability to check the joy that was overflowing in her.

At last the bell sounded. She flew to the door. But it was not Basil; it was Madame Blaquette. The landlady put her finger to her lips, glided quickly in, closed the door, and then, dropping her voice to a guilty whisper :

'Dear young lady,' she said, 'can I speak in the strictest privacy ?'

'Certainly, Madame Blaquette,' replied Narka, in a high, cheerful tone ; she was in a mood to enjoy the landlady's harmless little peculiarities.

'I have come to warn you of a great peril,' whispered Madame Blaquette, squeezing Narka's arm : 'the police have got notice that you have political papers here, and they are coming up to search your place. Burn or hide whatever you have ; but be quick ; there is no time to lose !'

Narka could hardly trust her senses. Was this a delusion, like the panic about the sewing-machine ? Still, she *had* those papers.

'Who told you the police were coming here ?' she asked.

'Dr. Schenk. He met me the other side of the Place, and sent me back to warn you. But make haste, or it will be too late!'

Narka's mistrust vanished at the mention of Schenk's name. She looked round her like a trapped creature seeking for some way of escape. There was none; there was no fire where she could burn the papers; and there was not a hole or corner in the narrow space where they would be safe for ten minutes from the lynx eyes of the police.

'I will take the papers and run down to the Sisters,' she said.

'Dear young lady, the police will meet you. They are coming up the street!'

'Then I am lost!' cried Narka, clasping her forehead with both hands.

There was sound of men's footsteps in the entry.

'Come,' she said; and seizing Madame Blaquette by the wrist, she drew her over to the alcove, dragged a box from under the bed, unlocked it, and took out the ivory casket which contained the papers and Basil's articles, and thrusting it into the landlady's hands, 'There! hide it under your shawl, and take it down to Sœur Marguerite for me.' There was a ring at the door. 'Oh, my God! there they are!' she cried, turning white to the lips.

'There is a back way, if I can get out through the kitchen window,' said Madame Blaquette; 'bring a chair!'

They hurried to the kitchen. Narka threw open the window, let down a chair, helped the agitated landlady to step on it, and then drew up the chair and shut the window, and went back into the room. The bell ran a second time. Narka, trembling in her strong young limbs, walked to the door and opened it.

'Oh, Marguerite, it is you! Come in quick,' she cried breathlessly.

And she told her in a few hurried words what had just happened.

'And she is gone down with the box to me?' said Marguerite; 'then I must hurry home, and be there to meet her.'

Narka would have been thankful to have the support of her presence when the police came ; but it was all-important to get the casket into safe-keeping, so she did not detain her.

Marguerite was not surprised on reaching the House to find that Madame Blaquette had not yet arrived : the back way made a great round, and the old lady had probably lingered to make sure of avoiding the police. The dispensary window commanded the court ; Marguerite went in there, so as to see her the moment she arrived. But ten minutes passed, and Madame Blaquette did not appear. Could she have been seen escaping from the window, and followed and arrested ? This was highly improbable ; still, when a quarter of an hour passed, Marguerite grew nervous. There was no one to consult. All the Sisters were absent on their rounds, or engaged in the schools. Suddenly the sound of a light hammer fell on her ear. She opened a door off the dispensary ; it was a closet into which they had smuggled

Antoine Drex. He was cobbling an old boot, nailing a sole to it. Antoine was safe as a tombstone, and cunning as a rat ; he knew the police, and he knew every turn of the lanes and courts through which Madame Blaquette had to pass. Marguerite told him what had happened.

'Most likely she's hiding till she makes sure those vermin are out of the way,' said Antoine. 'Keep your eye on the gate, ma sœur ; old Blaque will turn up.'

He nodded, and went on with his job ; but he knit his brow with a scowl.

'Take care you don't stay too long at that, Antoine,' said Marguerite ; 'the blood might go to your head, and bring on congestion.'

'Oh! I'm all right, ma sœur,' he replied, nodding confidentially.

Marguerite felt a little reassured. She went back into the dispensary, and kept her watch on the gate ; but when half an hour went by, and there was no sign of Madame Blaquette, she could bear it no longer. The suspense was intolerable. She resolved to

go back to Narka and see what had happened there, at any rate. She opened the
door of the closet to tell Antoine she was
going; but the place was empty. Where and
how had he gone off? She remembered
there was a way out by the garden, but he
must have got out of the window; and why
on earth had he done this? He was to have
made his escape that evening, travelling in a
wine waggon till he got to Caen, when he
was to be rolled off the truck, and to make
his way on foot to St. Aubin, his native
village. It seemed to Marguerite that everybody was on the wrong tack to-day. She
walked quickly back to Narka's. Her hand
shook as she pulled the bell, and she uttered
an exclamation of relief when Narka appeared.

'Well?'

'There has been nobody. I begin to
think Madame Blaquette imagined the whole
thing.'

'But the box? What has she done with
it?'

'The box? Hasn't she taken it to you?'

'No; she has never been near me.'

Narka turned deadly pale. A horrible suspicion flashed through both their minds.

'Oh, my God! it was a trap,' said Narka; 'it was a trap set for Basil! They must have tracked him here last night.'

The scared expression on Marguerite's face reminded Narka that she had not told her about Basil's arrival.

'Oh, darling!' she said, 'we have not had a moment to breathe, or I should have told you Basil has escaped: he is here in Paris. He came to see me last night; and I was expecting him again this morning when that dreadful woman came.'

'Basil is here!' Marguerite repeated, in blank amazement.

'Yes; he came late, about ten o'clock, and stayed till midnight; I watched him across the Place; there was not a soul about; but those bloodhounds must have tracked him!' She wrung her hands in misery.

They stood silent, both their hearts beating with terror.

'Do you know at all what those papers contained?' Marguerite asked, under her breath.

'I fancy they were a political programme, or something of that sort, drawn up by a man who is dead since, Ivan Gorff told me. But then there were those articles in Basil's own handwriting. Oh!'

Marguerite did not know what articles she was talking about; Narka had never told her of those translations, or of the meeting.

'Narka,' she said, laying her hand on the girl's arm, 'do you think there was a confession in them? *About Father Christopher?*'

'I don't think so; but I don't know. Oh, Marguerite, what is to be done?'

'Where is Basil staying?' asked Marguerite.

'I never thought of asking him. But Sibyl will know; he is most likely with her

now, if—— Oh, my God! I feel half mad!'
She put her hand to her forehead, and dropped
into a seat.

'We don't know yet whether he is caught,'
said Marguerite, 'or even likely to be caught;
don't let us jump at the worst conclusion in a
minute. The whole thing may be a silly
scare of that old goose Blaquette's invention.'

'But she said Schenk sent her to warn me.
How could she have known I had papers
unless he, or some one, told her?'

There was no denying this.

'Well, you can't sit here waiting to be
arrested,' said Marguerite. 'Put on your
bonnet, and go round by the back way and
take refuge with Madame Drex. And this
evening you can steal down to us.'

Narka heaved a great sigh, but she did not
move.

'Dear Narka, for Basil's sake don't lose
heart!' Marguerite entreated. 'Get up and
go, and I will hurry off to Sibyl.'

'Oh, Sibyl! Sibyl!' Narka cried, in an
accent of poignant pain.

'Go!' Marguerite persisted, trying to make her rise.

Narka seemed incapable either of resisting or deciding. She rose passively, and let Marguerite help on her bonnet and cloak.

'Let me see you safe out by the window before I go,' said Marguerite.

But Narka, roused at last to some realization of her position and of the necessity of the moment, said that she must put away some few things and lock her drawers. This was reasonable enough, and Marguerite, seeing that she had recovered her presence of mind, was satisfied to leave her behind and hurry off on her own mission. As they stood at the door together, Narka took her in her arms and kissed her, a long, loving kiss.

'God bless you, Marguerite! You are God's providence to me always.'

She opened the door to let her out. As she did so, two men stood outside. One was the Commissary of Police. He laid his hand on Narka's shoulder and said:

'I arrest you in the name of the Emperor!'

CHAPTER XVI.

THE PRIDE OF THE ZOROKOFFS.

SIBYL had returned to Paris the moment the riots were over; but she had not ventured near the disturbed quarters, nor had she seen Marguerite, consequently when the latter walked into her boudoir, half an hour after Narka's arrest, Sibyl welcomed her with double delight.

'You haven't met him!' she exclaimed, running to embrace her.

'Whom?' said Marguerite.

'Basil!—yes, *Basil!* He has only just left me. He is gone off to see you and Narka. He walked in here this morning, and nearly killed me with the joy of the surprise. You look as if you thought I had gone crazy ; but it is perfectly true.'

' I am only too glad to believe it,' replied Marguerite, with disappointing calmness. ' I am glad of good news from any direction.'

' Why, what do you mean ? What has happened ?' Sibyl asked, in alarm.

' Narka is in great trouble. She has been arrested.'

' Arrested ? Here ? Good heavens !' Sibyl sat down.

' Yes,' said Marguerite, sitting too ; ' it happened half an hour ago. I was there when the police came.'

' And what have they arrested her for ?'

Marguerite was embarrassed. If Basil had not spoken of his engagement, it might be indiscreet to mention the papers that had been seized.

' I heard nothing except that they had a warrant to arrest her,' she said. But the perplexity in her mind got into her face, and Sibyl saw it.

'You know more than that, Marguerite,' she said. 'Has Narka been associating with those wicked rioters up at La Villette ?'

'A man who was wounded and pursued by the police sought refuge with her one night, and that may have been discovered. But what is to be done ? How are we to help her ? You must know hosts of people who have influence ? There is Prince Krinsky ; you must go to him.'

'But he is the Russian Ambassador !'

'Well, and is not that a reason ? What are ambassadors for but to help their country-men when they get into trouble ?'

'That depends upon what the trouble is. It is not likely our Ambassador would feel it his duty to help any Russian for conspiring against our Emperor.'

'Why should you at once conclude that she has been conspiring against your Emperor ? My belief is, the whole affair is either a gross mistake or some cruel trick, and if you won't help her, I will ask Gaston to do it.'

'As if I did not care a great deal more

than Gaston about Narka!' retorted Sibyl.
'The fact is, I suspect I know more about
this arrest than you do. We were warned
months ago that Narka was associating with
disreputable people who would get her into
trouble. That Dr. Schenk that she had
attending her bears a very compromising
character. How came she to know him?'

'Through Ivan Gorff. Ivan brought him
to her when she fell ill. That was not her
fault.'

'It was her misfortune, anyhow. It obliged
me to be very circumspect in my intercourse
with her. It would not have done for me to
become identified with a person who associated with bad characters. My house is a
centre of Russian society in Paris, and though
I am now a Frenchwoman, it might have
injured my father and Basil if I had paraded
my friendship with a Russian who was on
intimate terms with conspirators.'

And so this was the *mot de l'énigme*, the
secret of the cold aloofness which had wounded
Narka so deeply.

' I don't believe Narka has been associating with conspirators,' said Marguerite. ' You need not have been afraid of her compromising you.' Then, after a moment's pause : ' What would they do to her if she were accused of anything of that sort ?'

' If she has mixed herself up in any treason against the Emperor of France, the French law would deal with her.'

' But if it was against the Emperor of Russia ?'

' In that case they would send her to Russia to be tried.'

' *Oh !*'

If Sibyl's answer had been, ' They will flog her to death,' the interjection could not have expressed more horror. Marguerite's look and tone seemed to hold a terrible revelation.

' Did Narka ever tell you about what happened to her in the prison ?' Sibyl asked in an altered manner.

' She let me guess. Oh, Sibyl!' said Marguerite, clasping her hands, and her eyes filled with tears, 'how awful if she were to go through that again !'

Sibyl changed colour, and stood up, and moved restlessly about the room. Then, as if conquered by some motive which bore down all opposition, 'I will go to Prince Krinsky,' she said.

Marguerite burst into tears, and kissed her. They talked the affair over rapidly, and then Marguerite, who had no time to lose, hurried away.

Sibyl ordered the carriage and went to dress. Just as she was ready to go downstairs, Basil came back with M. de Beaucrillon. They were both in high spirits.

'You have not heard ?' said Sibyl : 'Narka is arrested.'

Basil uttered a violent expletive in Russian, and turned pale.

'Arrested ! What for ?' said M. de Beaucrillon, scarcely less shocked.

'Marguerite, who told me about it—she has only just gone—says she knows nothing but the fact of the arrest. She was with

Narka when the police came and carried her away.'

'I must go to her at once,' said Basil, picking up his hat, which he had dropped in his excitement, and turning to leave the room ; 'I must go to the prison and pay my way in to her. Where is the prison ?'

'My dear Basil, you are the last person who ought to go near her,' protested Sibyl—'you, who are so compromised yourself.'

'Sibyl is right,' said M. de Beaucrillon. 'You would only compromise her still more. But what in Heaven's name has Narka been doing to get into this new trouble ?'

Basil took a turn in the room, and then, suddenly coming up to Sibyl, he said : 'The time has come for me to speak out : I am engaged to Narka.'

'*What ?*' Sibyl cried, almost with a shriek.

'*Diable !*' exclaimed M. de Beaucrillon.

Then followed a pause of stupefied amazement from both.

'Yes,' said Basil; 'the night I left Yrakow I asked her to be my wife. I cannot see why the news should strike you both dumb with horror, as if it were a crime. Narka is good, and gifted, and beautiful, and you, Sibyl, have looked on her as a sister all your life.'

But Sibyl could not answer him; the power of speech seemed to have left her. She was clutching the mantel, her face was blanched, the colour had faded from her eyes, and they stared fixedly at Basil with an expression that was indefinable.

'Mon cher ami,' said M. de Beaucrillon, 'I must own I don't understand your wonder at the effect of your announcement on my wife. It is not such a surprise to me. I always thought Narka's position in the family was an anomalous one, and likely to end in some catas—culmination of this sort. I said so to Sibyl long ago, but she ridiculed the idea and laughed at me.'

'I don't see why the culmination should have excited Sibyl's ridicule,' Basil retorted, looking angrily at her.

'One has not far to look for the reason, nevertheless,' said Gaston ; 'Mademoiselle Narka is undoubtedly all that you say, as gifted as she is good ; but she is the daughter of a Jewish trader, whereas you are——'

' Her affianced husband,' interrupted Basil.

' Ah ! just so. Then there is nothing more to be said, and it only remains for me to congratulate you.' And M. de Beaucrillon bowed stiffly.

' Oh, Basil ! Basil !' Sibyl cried, and she clasped her hands and burst into tears, and flung herself sobbing on a couch.

' So much for a woman's friendship !' said Basil bitterly ; and he looked at his brother-in-law as if expecting him to acquiesce in the masculine sneer ; but M. de Beaucrillon walked over and leaned against the chimney-piece, looking down at his sobbing wife with an air of unconcealed annoyance.

' Look here, Sibyl,' said Basil, after a momentary hesitation, ' and you too, de Beaucrillon, listen to what I have to say, and give me a fair hearing. When I came back that evening with Father Christopher's pardon, there was a warrant signed for my arrest : the Stanovoï gave me notice, and offered to let me escape before the warrant reached him if I paid him fifty thousand roubles. I could not by any possibility lay my hands on the sum within the time : I had three hours to find it. I knew you had not half the amount with you, and there was no one else to call upon. I was prepared to be arrested by ten o'clock that night. I told Narka about the warrant, and by mere chance I mentioned the offer made me by the Stanovoï. She gave me the money, and I escaped.'

' Narka !' they both exclaimed, aghast.

' Narka gave you *fifty thousand roubles !*' repeated M. de Beaucrillon, in a tone of dense incredulity.

' Narka,' replied Basil. ' It so happened that that very day she learned that a legacy of precisely fifty thousand roubles had been paid into the hands of Perrow for her by the executor of an uncle of Tante Nathalie. Narka rode in to X——, got the money, and returned just in time. The Stanovoï, who had had me closely watched, was lying in ambush at the gate, and I paid him the money. Before making my escape I asked Narka to be my wife.'

'Ma foi! I don't see how you could have helped it!' exclaimed M. de Beaucrillon, with generous warmth; 'no man of honour could have done less.'

'I don't see that at all,' said Sibyl, whose sobs and tears had been suddenly checked by the counter-current of emotion; 'I can't see that honour made it necessary for him to dishonour his family. It was most kind and generous of Narka; but any friend worthy of the name would have done as much. And, as far as that went, I would have paid the debt, had I known of it, within a month. I will do so now, and twofold, tenfold, gratefully and willingly.'

'There are debts that cannot be paid,' said Basil, angry and hurt; 'but the money is the least part of what I owe Narka.' He pulled at his moustache, and after a moment's wavering, 'I had in my possession at the time,' he continued, 'documents that were then of great importance, and of the most compromising character; I could not destroy them, and I dared not take them with me. I asked Narka to keep them. I knew, and she knew, that they would bring grievous trouble on anyone with whom they were found; but she accepted the trust without hesitating. The Stanovoï, who had seen her with me to the last, and who no doubt discovered that she had given me the ransom, denounced her as having my papers. She was arrested, and kept six months in prison. God and herself alone know what she suffered there; but they got nothing out of her. She left Kronstadt without having betrayed me by a word.' He stopped, overcome for a moment. 'You know the rest,' he went on hurriedly. 'Tante Nathalie could not rally from the shock. Narka came away amongst strangers, first in one place, then in another; she suffered every sort of hardship; and it has been all my doing. And because I don't

throw her over like a heartless scoundrel,
you cry out that I am dishonouring myself !'

'Narka is a noble creature,' said M. de
Beaucrillon, with genuine feeling. 'No man
worthy of the name could behave otherwise
than you are doing.'

Sibyl, who had entirely ceased crying, got
up and went over to Basil and kissed him.

'Yes, Narka has behaved nobly,' she said,
'and you are the most chivalrous of men.
For the sake of all she has done and suffered,
we will receive her as your wife.'

The concession was probably as much as
Basil ought to have expected from Sibyl
under any circumstances ; but he took it
coldly, and without a word of thanks or
comment.

'The question now is,' said M. de Beaucrillon, 'what is to be done to get her out of
this fresh trouble. You have no idea what
has led to it ?'

'I may still be the cause of it,' Basil
replied, remembering last night's visit, and

the possibility of its having been discovered.
'She may have kept those papers; it is very
possible.'

'Then we must go to Prince Krinsky at
once,' said Sibyl.

'What has Krinsky to do with it?' asked
Basil sharply.

'If she has been watched by our police—
and nobody else had any motive in watching
her--Prince Krinsky will know, and he is
the only person who can help.'

Basil thought it very unlikely that the
Prince would help; the name of Krinsky
had been as the seven devils let loose on him
all these months in St. Petersburg, and the
name of Zorokoff was no doubt in equally
bad odour with the Krinskys. The ambassador was not likely to extend his favour to
an offender identified with the family of the
man who had rejected Princess Marie.

'Sibyl is right,' said M. de Beaucrillon;
'Krinsky is the person we must apply to,
and no time must be lost.'

'I wish I could see Ivan before we move

in the matter,' said Basil, in evident perplexity. He went to the window, and saw
that the brougham was waiting in the court;
he pulled out his watch.

'I think I could catch him by driving there
now. Yes, I will try and see Ivan; he may
throw some light on the affair that will guide
us. Don't go to the Russian embassy till I
come back,' he said to Sibyl; and snatching
up his hat, he hurried away, and in a minute
they heard the brougham driving out of the
court.

'Well!' said M. de Beaucrillon, flinging
himself into a chair, and he threw up his
hands in a gesture of utter amazement; 'it is
the most astounding story that I ever heard!'

Sibyl tore off her bonnet and tossed it
from her, and pulled off her gloves in an
excited manner; she seemed too agitated to
speak. After a pause:

'To think,' she burst out, 'that Narka
should have been all this time engaged to
him, and never told me! The hypocrisy of
it is incredible. And to think of such a

scene going on that night at Yrakow, and I left in ignorance of it!'

'She showed extraordinary self-control, certainly,' said M. de Beaucrillon; 'very few women could have gone through such an ordeal without betraying themselves. And by heavens she does know how to love a man!' he added, in a tone of admiration that had a ring of envy in it.

'Better than she knows how to love a woman,' retorted Sibyl. 'To think that she could be so treacherous!'

Sibyl could not wish that Basil should be a scoundrel; but neither could she face the alternative. Surely, there must be some way out of the difficulty; surely, Providence would rescue the Zorokoffs from this shame, would save the holy place from that abomination of abominations, Jewish blood! She sat still, except for the nervous mechanical action of twisting her handkerchief into a rope, unconscious that her fingers were tearing the costly rag to shreds. The gong sounded, announcing a visitor.

'I hope no one is coming up here,' she said impatiently. 'Ring to forbid it.'

M. de Beaucrillon rang the bell which sounded the desired prohibition ; but before a servant could appear, Marguerite walked into the boudoir. They both greeted her with an exclamation of relief.

'Well, what news ?—have you seen her ?' asked Sibyl.

'No ; she has been before the Petit Parquet all the morning ; but one of the officials told me that she is to be taken from the dépôt to-night to St. Lazare.'

'Ah! then there is a true case against her ?' said Gaston : 'there will be a trial ?'

'Evidently. But I shall see Narka herself to-morrow.'

'Oh, Marguerite,' cried Sibyl, 'you don't know half the trouble ! Basil is engaged to her ! he is going to marry her !—*Narka !*'

Marguerite uttered something inarticulate, and blushed slowly.

'Yes, it is not to be believed,' protested Sibyl, misinterpreting the blush and the exclamation. 'And fancy her never breathing a word of it to any of us!—to *me*, that she pretended to love so! It is enough to make one loathe the whole race more than ever!'

M. de Beaucrillon shrugged his shoulders, and turned away with an impatient expletive.

'Perhaps Basil forbade her to tell,' Marguerite pleaded.

'Of course he did,' said M. de Beaucrillon, facing round. 'You talk like a fool, Sibyl! And what difference would it have made if she had told you? Would that have reconciled you to the marriage? Not a whit.'

'I should have felt that she had behaved loyally to me.'

'Bah! Her loyalty was due to Basil; and she has proved it right nobly. The only pity is she's not a Narichkin or a Woronsoff. But I forgot,' said he, turning to Marguerite, 'you have not heard the story yet.'

And he told her briefly of the ransom, the

flight, the papers left with Narka, and the trouble they had brought upon her.

' Oh, Sibyl ! is it any wonder that Basil loves her ?' Marguerite pleaded. ' How could he have done less than make her an offer of his hand ?'

' Perhaps not,' replied Sibyl ; ' but Narka took an unworthy advantage in accepting it. She knew the offer was made in a moment of extraordinary excitement, under almost overpowering pressure of motives ; an honourable woman would have said, " Wait a year, and then, if you are of the same mind, ask me again." '

' I wonder how many men would have been of the same mind at the end of a year ?' said Marguerite, with a toss of her head.

M. de Beaucrillon looked at her in amused surprise.

' You little sceptic, where did you get your estimate of us, I should like to know ? I dare say you are right enough, though,' he added. ' All the same, I'm not sure but that the ficklest amongst us would prefer the

woman who took him at his word; the
woman who loved him would be sure to
do that; and Narka loves Basil, and no
mistake.'

'Then, if she loves him, she must do him
good,' said Marguerite. 'Oh, Sibyl! won't
you remember all she has suffered for Basil's
sake, and try to love her?'

'I have got first to try to forgive her,'
Sibyl replied coldly.

She looked as cold and hard as if she had
been turned to ice.

Marguerite had been prepared for a great
deal, but the sight of this frozen hardness
under that soft, smiling, sympathetic exterior
shocked her inexpressibly.

'What is there to be done?' she said,
addressing her brother: 'Prince Krinsky
will help, will he not?'

'We don't know that yet,' replied Gaston.
'If, as we fear—as Basil fears—the trouble
comes from meddling with Russian politics,
the Russian ambassador may refuse to
interfere.'

' But he has a wife, a daughter ? Princess
Marie, who is young, surely she will be kind ?
Go to her, Sibyl, and tell her everything !
Tell her that Basil loves Narka, and is
engaged to be married to her.'

Sibyl gave a little sardonic laugh.

' That would not be the way to touch her ;
no woman cares to help the rival who has
supplanted her. Marie would hate Narka ;
in her place, any girl would, unless she were
an angel.'

' And why should she not be an angel ?
Nothing makes angels or devils of people
like believing them to be such. Go to Marie
as if you believed she was an angel ; tell her
everything, and trust to her pity and gene-
rosity. Dear Sibyl, do !'

While Marguerite pleaded and entreated,
Sibyl seemed to be rapidly debating the
question in her own mind ; she was looking
fixedly out of the window, her features
agitated, her hands nervously moving in that
unconscious, mechanical twisting of her handkerchief. Suddenly her brow cleared, like a

person who sees a way out of a difficulty, and has determined to follow it.

'Yes, you are right,' she said ; 'that is the best thing to do. We must wait till Basil comes back, as we promised him, and if he has no reason for preventing it, I will go at once to Marie, and try if she is of the stuff that angels are made of.'

Marguerite had now done all that was possible for the moment ; so, promising to let them know when she had seen Narka, she went away.

M. de Beaucrillon, observant of the courtesies which French gentlemen never fail in to the women of their family, saw her downstairs, and then returned to the boudoir. He was struck immediately by the change that had taken place in Sibyl. The strained, angry, perplexed look had entirely passed away from her countenance, and it now wore a resolute, almost a radiant expression. Was it the hope of saving Narka from a horrible fate that had suddenly flushed her pale cheeks, and lighted those lamps of triumph in her eyes? What else could it be?

And yet, for the first time, as he looked at his wife, M. de Beaucrillon did not think Sibyl beautiful.

CHAPTER XVII.

IN THE VISION OF THE NIGHT.

NARKA was alone in her cell at St. Lazare. No one had been to see her. She had waited and watched all the long day. Every step echoing on the stone corridor made her pulses quicken with hope : it might be Marguerite, or Sibyl, or even Basil. But the day dragged on to its close, the bars and bolts of the prison were drawn, and no one came.

Narka had not slept the previous night, and she had hardly tasted food since her arrest ; she was physically exhausted, and her nerves were strained and excited to the verge of delirium. When the night closed in, she was in the state of one prepared to see visions.

For a while, the lamp burning outside sent a tawny light into her cell through the window above the door; but this was put out, and then all was black as the tomb, and a horror of great darkness fell upon her. She could not say how long it lasted, until suddenly, the external blackness was pierced through by a vivid inward illumination. Her whole life, from childhood to the present hour, passed before her, with its sorrows, its blighted hopes, its pathetic failures; every circumstance became invested with a high prophetic meaning, every cruel and humiliating event grew instinct with a supreme significance, every incident pointed to momentous issues. Her faith, hitherto a sort of dreamy mysticism, gradually kindled to a fervour of frenzy, that she mistook for inspiration. She saw the divine scheme for the redemption of humanity unfolding before her like a scroll, and she read her own part

distinctly written there. God, who had
created and redeemed every individual soul,
could not overlook the very least of His
creatures ; with Him, there was neither
greater nor lesser; the monarch on his throne
and the moudjik in his hovel were of equal
value in His sight; the same hand which
fashioned the eagle, and bid it soar and fix
the mid-day sun, also created the worm, and
bade it crawl upon the earth ; and both were
His creatures, equally entitled to His care.
It was, nevertheless, in the order of His
providence that amongst men there should
be higher and lower; that some should play
a grand part in life, and some an obscure
one; that some should command and enjoy,
and even sin with impunity, while others
were condemned to suffer for the sins of all.
And these latter were His chosen partners
in the plan of redemption. They were to
enter into glory with Him through suffering,
and become like unto gods.

As the symbolism of her destiny revealed
itself to Narka, her heart swelled with a

sense of vengeful triumph. She exulted in her Christ-like mission, and in spirit trampled under foot the Pharisees and tyrants who persecuted her. She saw her own name written on the roll of martyrs, while angels clothed her in crimson, and placed the palm-branch in her hand, in presence of the rejoicing hierarchies. How weak and cowardly it would be to count the cost of such a destiny! The night wore on in this frenzy of pride and hallucination. The prison clock told away the hours. The dawn broke; but in the cell all was still dark. Suddenly, a gleam of light crept in through the window above the door, and Narka, looking up as if something had touched her, saw the white Figure of the crucifix, alone visible in the encircling blackness.

'Yes,' she said within herself, 'it is we who can look down from our gibbet on the children of this world, the fools who feast and revel, while we agonize with Christ in His passion! To us, instead of ashes, He will give a crown, and a garment of glory

for an afflicted spirit. Those who have
dwelt in the tombs shall rejoice and sing
canticles, while those who have slept in
palaces on pillows of down shall howl ior
grief, and rend their garments!'

In the weird, shadowy dawnlight, her
thoughts grew concrete, and took tangible
form. She saw a long procession marching
past : victors and saints who had blessed
their generation, and left the world better
than they found it ; but they were not the
prosperous ones whose course had been
through flowery meads, full of sunshine and
peace ; they were men who had suffered,
who had known poverty, humiliation, and
defeat ; never since the beginning of the
world had a nation's wrong been made right,
or a people's sorrow consoled, by the rich
and the satisfied, by those who had gone
through life making merry, crowned with
flowers, and sung to and smiled upon ;
these conquests had been achieved by
pilgrims who toiled through the desert in
hunger and thirst and nakedness, or by

martyrs who walked over the fiery plough-
shares.

Narka had always vaguely held that suffering was in itself an agency of redemption,
and meritorious apart from all merit or response in the sufferer. This old creed was
now asserting itself with the passionate
intensity which belongs rather to fanaticism
than to faith. She looked upon herself as
a victim for her people, an object of complacency to the court of heaven. Her mind,
her senses, her heart, inflamed by these stern
and sanguine orthodoxies, all shared the
intoxication of the vision they had conjured
up.

But in this splendid apotheosis, where she
was the central figure, she was not alone—
Basil Zorokoff was by her side, he was
whispering in her ear; every fibre of her
heart was thrilling to what he whispered;
she felt his breath upon her cheek, she felt
the warm clasp of his arm round her. Ah!
let fate do its worst upon her; with that
arm clasping her, she could never be wholly

miserable. But suddenly the smile of rapture
that trembled on her lips died away. What
fool's paradise had she wandered into ? . . .
She was in prison, and so, perhaps, was Basil,
for all she knew. There was that box containing the articles in his handwriting ! If
the writing should be traced ? Narka
shuddered, but, quickly dismissing the horrible
thought, she remembered that Basil was in
France, and that his own Government could
not touch him, and the French police were
not likely to be able to identify the writing of
a Russian.

The great clock struck five, and the profound stillness began to be broken by those
sounds which announce, even in a prison,
that the inmates are awakening to the
activities of life. Warders came and went
along the flagged passages, doors were
opened and shut, the bell summoned the
prisoners to the scant morning meal. Narka
was not in the category of those who had
to obey its call. Her food was brought to
her. She was too faint and feverish to feel

any appetite ; but she knew that this was
partly the effect of hunger, so she ate a few
mouthfuls, and went back to her visions.

The morning wore on. It was near noon,
and she was still sitting on the edge of her
bed, listless, tired, her mind strained between
something like ecstasy and stupor, when
the door of her cell opened, and some one
pronounced her name. She started, stood
straight up, and felt herself clasped in
Sibyl's arms.

' Basil ?' she said, in a frightened whisper,
as, disengaging herself, she fixed her passionate, yearning eyes on Sibyl.

' He has told us everything.'

'And you forgive me? You forgive us
both ?'

' Forgive you ! My brave, generous
Narka, what have I to forgive ?'

And Sibyl kissed her again tenderly, cling-
ingly, and then she drew her to the bed, and
they sat down together.

Narka was crying ; it was an immense
relief both to her nerves and her heart, and

Sibyl let the tears flow on, wiping them away gently with her own little cambric handkerchief, and kissing the heavy white lids between whiles. But Narka was not one to indulge long in the luxury of emotion. She drew a deep breath, and then, lifting her head from Sibyl's shoulder :

'Tell me what has happened,' she said. ' Has he been arrested ?'

'Who ? Basil ? No. Did you hear that he had been ?'

'I have heard nothing. I have seen nobody. I thought Marguerite would have come.'

'She has been trying to get to see you from the first ; but they made difficulties. Gaston saw the president of the Petit Parquet this morning.'

'Ah ! And what did he tell him ? About the articles in that box ? Do they know who wrote them ?'

'They have not got the box. It seems that, as the detective was carrying it off, a man fell upon him and knocked him

down, and seized it and made away with
it.'

'Oh! Who was the man, did they say?'

'He was a rebel, who had been wounded
in the head during the *émeute*. Gaston did
not hear his name.'

'It was Antoine Drex!' Narka exclaimed,
with sudden elation.

'Oh, Narka!' said Sibyl, shocked at what
seemed to her like cynical complacency in
the disreputable circumstances; 'what could
have induced you to mix yourself up with
those low men and their politics?'

'I did not mix myself up with them,' protested Narka. 'I have never meddled in
their politics here. Why should I?'

'But you have meddled in Russian politics.
They say you have been associating with the
worst revolutionists, and frequenting their
meetings. They say you were at one on the
10th where a plot was discussed for murdering our Emperor.'

'That is a lie. I was not there. And if
I had been, I should certainly have not

voted for such an insane crime as that.
What stupidity ! What good could it do
to murder the Emperor ? Who could have
said I was there ? Not that it matters.
Even if I had been, I am in a foreign
country, and beyond the reach of Russian
tyranny. Their slanders can't touch me
here.'

' Dear, you are mistaken,' said Sibyl, with
a certain tender hesitation ; 'if it is proved,
or even asserted on good authority, that you
have been mixed up with the revolutionary
movement, the Russian law will reach you
here just as surely as if you were at home.'

' How so ?' Narka started perceptibly.

' If the Russian authorities demand it, our
ambassador will be obliged to claim you as a
Russian subject.'

' What do you mean ?' said Narka, turning
a white face to her.

' Dearest, did you not know ? As a Russian subject, guilty of high-treason, you will
be handed over to our ambassador, and taken
back to be tried in Russia.'

Sibyl was not so certain that this was true ; she believed it was, because she wanted it to be true ; it was so essential to her success that it *must* be true, and she spoke with the quiet assurance of one whose knowledge rested on the most undoubted authority.

Narka stared at her, every feature convulsed, while a cold chill of horror stole the heat out of her blood.

' *They will send me back to Russia ?*' she murmured, in a voice that sounded like a whisper in the dark. Her lips fell slowly apart ; there came a blackness under her eyes as if they suddenly reflected some invisible spectacle of woe or horror; her hands opened and closed nervously, and then crept slowly up and coiled round her neck ; she presented an image of terror and despair awful to behold.

Sibyl watched her with intensely curious, but not unpitiful eyes : she pitied her sincerely, but she pitied herself more ; she wanted to save Narka, but she wanted first to save Basil and the pride of the Zorokoffs.

The moment had now come, she thought, for proposing the only expedient which might do this. She laid her hand on Narka's tense arm; it shuddered under the touch.

'This is what I have dreaded from the moment I heard of your being arrested,' she said; 'I lay awake all last night thinking how I could save you, and praying to God to show me a way. For, Narka, there is no use in trying to deceive ourselves: you will be handed over to the Russian Government and taken to St. Petersburg, and then . . . But, darling, there is one chance still of saving you. I know not how to propose it, for the sacrifice will be almost worse than the sacrifice of your life.'

Narka did not make a sign, but sat staring at vacancy, her eyes still riveted on that unseen horror.

'Beloved,' continued Sibyl, in a low, caressing voice, 'if you are sent back to Russia, it means Kronstadt '—a tremor ran through Narka—'or Siberia; in either case a fate as cruel as death; and you are parted

from Basil for ever. If you give him up
voluntarily now, you will remain free, and you
will be still his sister and mine.'

Narka did not speak, but she moved her
head imperceptibly towards Sibyl ; the movement seemed to say, ' What do you mean ?'

Sibyl stole one arm round her neck, and
speaking rapidly :

' Oh, my darling,' she said, ' if I could take
the sting out of the sacrifice for you ! . . .
but the alternative is so horrible it will give
you courage : Renounce Basil ; tell him you
have ceased to care for him ; that you will
not marry him, because you don't love him.
He will then be free to go and offer himself
to Prince Krinsky's daughter, and ask her to
obtain your release.'

Narka was moved at last from her stony
immobility. She slowly drew away her hands
from about her neck, and looked at Sibyl.

' *Tell him that I do not love him ?*' she
repeated. ' He would not believe me ; he
would know that it was a lie.'

' He knew it once, dear ; but you may have

changed since then. How many women would! Remember, it is nearly two years since you have met?'

'It is not three days! I saw him here before you did. He came to me the moment he arrived in Paris, and he knows whether or not I have ceased to love him! Yes, he knows; he knows that I love him with my whole soul; that to give him up would be to me worse than death, worse than Kronstadt!'

Her eyes, a moment ago fixed and lifeless, grew suddenly incandescent as they met Sibyl's, glittering with fury.

'So you have been deceiving me to the very last!' Sibyl cried, with a light laugh that sounded horrid; 'while I have been watching and praying, and straining every nerve to save you, you have been playing the hypocrite, spreading your toils round my brother! You living lie! You false friend! You companion of men who plot murder! You base, guilty woman!'

'Guilty?' repeated Narka, and she rose to her feet, no longer the cowed, terror-stricken

creature of a moment ago, but a grand,
passionate woman, strong in her innocence,
and conscious of being set, by her sufferings,
high above this proud daughter of princes—
'guilty? Look at that symbol!' She laid
one hand fiercely on Sibyl's arm, and with
the other pointed to the white Figure on the
wall : 'We shall both of us be judged by It,
condemned or acquitted according to the
likeness we bear to It. Which of us, you or
I, as we stand here, most resembles *Him?*
Is it you, with your wealth, your splendour,
and your high place in this world, your feast-
ing and purple and fine linen, your pampered
ease? or I, in humiliation and poverty, in my
body seamed with scars, marked and cut with
the hangman's lash'—Sibyl shrank from her
with a low cry, and hid her face—'with my
heart pierced by the murder of my kindred ;
with my soul made sorrowful to death by the
sufferings of my people, and the sight of the
wrongs inflicted on them by you and your
caste? Is it I, in imprisonment and per-
secution, in the martyr's death that perhaps

awaits me? . . . Let the Christ speak, and say which of us two is guilty, which of us two deserves that glance of recognition reserved to those who here below have been likened to the Man of Sorrows !'

Narka had begun in a husky, agitated voice, but as she went on it rose, under the stress of irrepressible emotion, to high vibrating tones. As she stood, pointing to the Figure on the cross, Sibyl almost expected to hear a voice resound in the dark cell, uttering the awful sentence of acquittal and denunciation : 'Come, ye blessed !— Depart, ye accursed !'

'Narka! Narka!' she cried, cowering before the terrible wrath of the woman she had scorned a moment ago, and who now stood like the avenger of the brethren accusing her before the judgment-seat; 'why do you curse me? I have not done those things; I had no hand in the murder of your kindred, or in the sorrows that have come upon you. I have loved you always; but you broke away from me; you turned against us, and took part with those who hate us. Why did not you trust me? I wanted to save you— God knows I did—and you upbraid me as if I had been seeking to destroy you!'

But Sibyl too had had her hour of exaltation. Her nerves, taxed to their utmost by the strain of the last three days, broke down, and she burst into a fit of hysterical weeping.

Narka seemed hardly conscious of her presence. Her whole soul was torn asunder by this choice that was thrust upon her, of renouncing Basil, or going back to encounter again those horrors of which she had never before spoken to any human being.

The hour struck without either of them hearing it; but it was a relief to both when the warder came and said it was time for Sibyl to come away.

When the door had closed upon her, Narka flung herself upon the bed, and her bursting heart once more found relief in a passionate flood of tears.

CHAPTER XVIII.

PENDING THE TRIAL.

WHEN Basil went in search of Ivan on the morning of Narka's arrest, he heard that his friend had left town, and, as usual, without saying where he was going, or when he would return. Basil went every day to the house to inquire, and on the fourth day, late in the afternoon, he walked into Ivan's room, and found him smoking a pipe, and reading the newspaper.

'You have not heard what has happened?' said Basil, guessing from his quiet air and occupation that he knew nothing.

'What?' said Ivan, removing his pipe, and opening his eyes in hilarious curiosity.

'Narka has been arrested. She has been four days in prison.'

Ivan dropped the newspaper with an oath.

Basil related all he knew of the event. 'Who has done it?' he said. 'Can it be Schenk?'

Ivan did not answer. He laid his clenched hands on his knees, and bent forward. He knew of Schenk's passion for Narka, and Olga Borzidoff knew it; she had complained bitterly to Ivan of Schenk's unfaithfulness, and she was a violent, vindictive woman, whose jealousy would be unscrupulous. If Schenk had let out the fact that Narka had documents in her possession, Olga would not have hesitated to use the knowledge in order to destroy her. There was no use, however, in confiding these suspicions to Basil.

'Schenk has never done it,' he said; 'he is not capable of it; but he may have been fool enough to let out something that compromised her. If he has, he deserves the knout!' Ivan ground his teeth with a sinister sound. 'But the thing is, what is to be done for her? Your sister must have interest at

Court. She will use it, won't she ? Napoleon,
for all he is a despot, has a man's heart, and
can be pitiful, and the Empress is a woman.'

'That won't help, if it can be proved that
Narka has been mixed up in our work. If
they accuse her of offending against the
French law, well and good ; the people here
may help ; but if not, there is no one but
Krinsky who could do it, and in that case my
sister must go to him at once.'

'She can't go to him to-day, nor to-morrow
either ; he left Paris last night for Berlin.'

'Confound it! did he ?' said Basil, turning suddenly round. 'And when is he to be
back ?'

'I don't know. He is to stop at Berlin
two days, and then, unless his business is
arranged at once with Bismarck, he will go on
to St. Petersburg.'

'Have you any idea when the trial is likely
to come on ?' asked Basil.

'I don't suppose before a month at least.'

'And they will keep her in prison all that
time untried ?'

'Yes. They have got their *prison pré-ventive* here like us, for all their boasted liberty and justice. But it will serve a good purpose for once by giving Krinsky time to be back before the trial comes on.'

Basil said nothing for a moment. Then, 'We can't wait for Krinsky to come back,' he said; 'I must start after him at once, and secure him before he leaves for St. Petersburg. If I take the express to-night, I am safe to catch him at Berlin. I shall be able to get to see him through Z——, of our embassy there. He is not a bad fellow, and though my father made a mess between him and me, I don't believe he is as savage against me as they made out. Anyhow, there is nothing else to be done. I will drive now to Sibyl's, and tell her I am off.' He pulled out his watch : 'It is five o'clock ; I have a couple of hours to do a few things, and eat a mouthful before I start.'

Basil hurried away, hailed a cab, and drove to the Rue St. Dominique.

Sibyl was out. She had left home three

hours ago, the servant said, so was likely to
be soon back.   But Basil could not wait.
He went into the library, and wrote a note to
M. de Beaucrillon, telling him of his departure
for Berlin, and the motive of it.

Sibyl, meantime, had gone to make a call
at the Russian embassy, and had learned
to her disappointment that the Prince had
left the night before for Berlin, and the ladies
for Fontainebleau that morning.

As she drove in under her own gateway,
M. de Beaucrillon's brougham was moving
away from before the steps of the house.   He
met her in the hall with two letters in his
hand.   One was Basil's, the other was from
Marguerite.

'Come in here a moment,' he said, and
they went into the library.   'Here is a slate
on our heads!' he exclaimed : 'Basil is off to
Berlin after Krinsky, and Marguerite tells me
the trial comes on on Monday.   It may be
all over before Basil will have seen Krinsky.
Though, for the matter of that, we don't
know yet whether Krinsky can be of any use.'

Sibyl took the two notes from his hand without speaking. There is an electric, instantaneous comprehension that comes to the brain in moments of supreme excitement, and enables it to seize all the points of a question, and arrive at a conclusion without any process of argument. Such a moment had come to Sibyl now. With one glance, she saw the whole situation, the circumstances, the possibilities. Basil's absence at this crisis was providential. The trial would be over, perhaps, before he heard it had begun, and there was an end of the terror which had haunted her of his appearing in court and publicly compromising himself from a sense of chivalrous loyalty to Narka.

' I must see at once about getting counsel,' said M. de Beaucrillon, too selflessly absorbed in Narka's trouble and the impending crisis to stop to consider the motive of his wife's silence. ' There is no time to lose. I will go at once to Maître X——. If I am late for dinner, don't wait for me.'

CHAPTER XIX.

IN COURT.

IT was not often that so great a treat as this trial of Narka's was provided for the sensation-loving Parisian public. The prisoner was a young girl of rare beauty and brilliant gifts, and among the witnesses were to figure a *grande dame* and a Sister of Charity.

The court was densely filled long before the entrance of the judge; but curiosity reached its climax when the door opposite the judgment-seat opened, and the prisoner, walking between two gendarmes, was led to the bar.

Narka had been so exhausted and strained

by the week's imprisonment that, on the eve,
it had seemed to her impossible she could go
through the ordeal of this trial ; but when
the morrow came, and with it the challenge
for immediate effort, her splendid young
vitality asserted itself, and her high courage
rose to the occasion. She was luminously
pale, but there was no lack of fire in her eyes,
and no trace of weakness in her bearing, as
she stood at the bar. A murmur, partly of
admiration, partly of curiosity, rose from every
part of the audience ; but this quickly subsided,
and profound silence reigned in the court.

The case against the prisoner was briefly
stated : from the time of her arrival in Paris
she had consorted with conspirators of
various nationalities, and attended revolutionary meetings where plots were hatched
against the governments and the lives of
kings ; she had gone to live in a district
where disaffection was rampant ; she had
received treasonable documents, and shel-
tered ringleaders of the recent *émeute*, notoriously bad characters, etc.

After this preliminary discourse, the judge
proceeded to examine the prisoner, to inquire
her name, her parentage, her present circumstances, putting her through that minute and
elaborate legal inquisition which assumes that
the court has not the most remote idea who
the prisoner is, where he comes from, or
what has brought him to the bar.

Narka gave her answers in a firm, distinct
voice which betrayed no weakness of emotion.
Perhaps this was because she felt none ;
absolute despair had made her stoical : in
ceasing to hope, she ceased to tremble.   She
had come here prepared to meet the worst ;
not merely death, but that worse fate which
awaited her if she was handed over to the
Russian authorities.   She was still in the
dark as to the probabilities of this alternative.
If she was convicted to-day of active partici-
pation in a plot to assassinate the Emperor
of the French, she would, no doubt, be condemned to the guillotine.   This was the best
fate she could hope for.   She did hope for it.

A great orator once said, ' L'homme qui

veut mourir est toujours le maître de l'homme qui veut vivre.' Narka was conscious of holding this supreme command over the mass of humanity whose hungry curiosity was devouring her humiliation. There was probably not one man in all that crowd who despised death as she did, who would have faced it so fearlessly ; and this proud sense of superiority, real or imaginary, helped to keep her pulses steady, and her voice from faltering.

The judge, involuntarily perhaps, paid her that tribute of respect which high courage commands under all circumstances. He questioned her searchingly, but his manner from first to last was civil. Narka came through the ordeal without having damaged her cause by an imprudent avowal, or a weak denial. The examination, if it did not prove anything, impressed the court personally in her favour.

The first witness called up was Olga Borzidoff. She swore that the prisoner had to her knowledge habitually frequented revolutionary meetings, and that on the 10th instant she had been present at one where a scheme for the assassination of the Emperor of the French had been arranged, and the prisoner was chosen by lots to give the signal for throwing the bomb-shell into his carriage; the witness had been so horrified by the proceedings and plans discussed at this meeting that she had gone immediately and given warning to the police; she had herself assisted at former meetings of the sort, ignorant of their sinister character; but her eyes had been opened on this occasion, and her conscience awakened. Olga Borzidoff deposed in a spirit of vindictive personal rancour which greatly damaged the weight of her evidence, and, at last, she became so violent and aggressive that the judge was obliged to call her to order.

Madame Blaquette was next called up, and came on whining and whimpering, and conveying her distress to Narka by side-glances and gesticulations. She gave her evidence incoherently, contradicting herself at every

sentence ; she had been beguiled and deceived, she said, by a beggar-woman towards
whom she had exercised benevolence to the
utmost extent of her means, having on one
occasion given the last penny she possessed
to relieve her wants ; the woman's ingrati-
tude was a bitter drop in the cup of her
manifold disappointments. The landlady
was wandering on to explain the nature of
these disappointments, when the judge cut
her short, and after a series of direct questions discharged her. Her evidence had
neither served nor hurt Narka.

Several other witnesses, friends of Olga
Borzidoff, were heard, and these swore to the
prisoner's presence at the meeting on the
10th. This testimony was, so far, the only
substantial charge against her. Then the
counsel for the Crown made his charge, and
the witnesses for the defence followed.

The first called was the Comtesse de
Beaucrillon. Sibyl was one of those persons
whose charm never deserts them under any
circumstances. As she advanced now to the

witness-box, leaning on her husband's arm,
she looked just as charming, just as much at
her ease, as if she had been taking part in a
Court ceremonial, or dispensing cups of tea
in her boudoir. She sat down with that
languishing grace which always suggested a
nymph sinking into the water, and then drew
off her gloves, and pulled out her Lilliputian
handkerchief, scattering a scent of violets
that perfumed deliciously the heavy air
around her.

After the preliminary formula of questions,
the judge said :

' How long have you known the prisoner ?'

' All my life, monsieur. We were brought
up together ; we studied together ; we were
like sisters.'

' The prisoner is charged with having
become acquainted with revolutionists, and
been cognizant of plots against the life of the
Emperor of Russia, even while under the
roof of Princess Zorokoff.'

' Ah ! Monsieur le Président, such charges
are wicked slanders. My sister Narka was

too pure and good to associate with any but those who were pure and good like herself.'

There was an indescribable charm in the way Sibyl said 'my sister Narka,' in her softly agitated voice.

'Madame,' continued the judge, 'the court cannot accept sentimental evidence, however convincing it may be. Can *you* assert upon your oath that, to your knowledge, the prisoner never associated, was never in communication, while in Russia, with any persons disaffected toward the imperial government?'

Sibyl seemed too horrified to answer. With a marvellous play of feature she looked up at her husband, and clasping her hands nervously, looked back at the judge.

'Am *I* suspected of being disaffected to the Emperor's government?'

Nothing could have been more perfect than the little bit of comedy; her face and her hands expressed amazement, amusement, and wounded loyalty all at once, and the pantomime told more effectively in Narka's behalf than if Sibyl had solemnly sworn to belief in her innocence.

'You, madame, are absolutely above suspicion,' protested the judge, feeling that he had made a mistake in rousing the sympathies of the public on the side of this sensitive, high-bred lady by inferentially accusing her of a vulgar crime.

Sibyl saw her advantage, and immediately the great crystal drops welled up into her light blue eyes and trembled there, and then rolled off her curled lashes. She was one of those dangerous, not-to-be-trusted women to whom tears are becoming, and she knew it.

'I beg your pardon, M. le Président,' she said, her voice quivering with repressed emotion; 'but if you have ever had a sister whom you loved and trusted with your whole heart, you will understand that I cannot listen unmoved to such horrible insinuations against mine.'

Overcome by her feelings, she covered her face and sobbed gently.

A hum of admiration and respect made itself heard in the court.

Sibyl, after struggling for a moment with her emotion, lifted her head with the air of one nerving herself for courageous effort, but the judge, obeying the murmured desire of the court, said :

'The witness may retire. Let Sœur Marguerite be heard.'

No more striking contrast could have been found than that which this witness presented to the last. Instead of the *blonde élégante*, trailing her silken skirts with undulating grace, scattering the scent of violets around, and playing on the court with her wiles, her sudden tears, her harmonies and blandishments, there appeared at the bar a small, well-shaped young woman clothed in a gray woollen gown and a broad white head-gear, from under which there looked out a youthful face with irregular features, a nose full of character, imperceptibly *retroussé*, and a pair of wistful brown eyes alight with courage, simplicity and truth. The shapely hands,

roughened with work and the weather, were
slipped into her wide sleeves, and Marguerite
in the witness-box looked like a diligent little
scholar who came up for examination, primed
and loaded, afraid of nothing except of being
confused into a wrong answer from nervous-
ness.

'What is your name?' asked the judge.

'Sœur Marguerite, M. le Juge.'

'Say M. le Président,' corrected some one
in a *sotto voce.*

'Pardon! M. le Président,' she repeated
with a blush.

The usual interrogations followed, and then
the judge said :

'Why did the prisoner go to live at La
Villette?'

'Because it is cheap, M. le Président.'

'How did she spend her time there, do
you know?'

'She gave lessons, M. le Président ; and
she went about with me visiting the sick poor.
She is a capital sick-nurse.'

'Did she not keep low company?'

'She kept company with me, M. le Président.'

'You know what I mean, ma sœur; she associated with the bad characters of the place?'

'So do I and my sisters, M. le Président.'

'Vive Sœur Marguerite!' shouted a voice, and the cry was taken up in chorus at the end of the hall, where La Villette was largely represented.

The judge turned round angrily; but before he could speak, Marguerite drew her hand from her sleeve, and made a little downward gesture, as if she were slapping a naughty child.

'Hush, will you!' she cried; 'do you want to get me into trouble?'

This irregular proceeding had the desired effect, so the judge overlooked it, and went on:

'You are acquainted with a man named Antoine Drex?'

'Yes, M. le Président; I have long been acquainted with Antoine Drex.'

' He bears a detestable character : a rioter,
a drunkard ; he was a notoriously bad
husband ; he used to beat his wife ?'

Marguerite put her head first a little to
one side, then a little to the other, like a
meditative robin.

' Well, M. le Président, he was not a model
husband ; but his wife was very aggravating;
she had a tongue that was going all day long ;
and she took to drink before he did. Our
sisters always pitied Antoine very much.'

' What ! a wicked revolutionist who incited
the people to bloodshed ?'

' M. le Président, he was not so bad as
that; c'était un désespéré, mais pas un révolté.
That is the difference. When he was out of
work and had no food, the hunger went to
his head. It is so with them all. But he
was not a bad fellow ; he loved his mother,
and was always good to her ; and he would
often share his crust with a hungry
neighbour.'

' So would any man who was not a brute.'

' Ah ! M. le Président, if that were true,

there would be no *émeutes.* It is hunger that sends the *ouvrier* down into the street. He is not wicked ; he is a good fellow if you give him bread enough ; but he goes mad on an empty stomach, and that hunger-madness is the worst of all !'

There was a murmur in the court expressing horror and assent.

' That is a subject that would carry us too far from the point in question, ma sœur,' said the judge : 'the question is, did the prisoner, knowing the character Antoine Drex bears, associate with him, and connive at his evil doings by hiding him from the pursuit of the law ?'

' M. le Président, I cannot answer for the other people who hid Antoine from the police ; but I don't deny that we did. He came to us one morning and asked us to shelter him, and we let him in, and he went away without telling us.'

' Yes, he went away to intercept the police, who had just got possession of a box containing papers that would have convicted the

prisoner beyond any doubt. Ma sœur, do
you know what those papers were ?'

'No, I do not ; I never saw them ; and
Mademoiselle Larik never told me what they
were.'

'You know that she held revolutionary
doctrines, and connived at, if she did not
participate in, the crime of regicide ?'

'I know nothing of the sort, and I don't
believe a word of it.'

'She frequented meetings where such plots
were discussed ?'

'If she did, it must have been as the
prophet Daniel frequented the lions' den :
she was taken there by force or by fraud.
But I don't believe she was ever present at
such a meeting.'

'There are witnesses to swear that she was
present at one where she was designated as
an accomplice in an attempt on the life of the
Emperor.'

'Monsieur le Président, if a court full of
witnesses swore to that, I would not believe
them.'

' How if they proved it, ma sœur ?'

' Above all, if they proved it ! What a
pitiful sort of faith that must be that could be
invalidated by proofs !'

There was a laugh in the court. The
judge peered over his spectacles at the
witness, as if debating whether to join, at
least tacitly, in the *mouvement d'hilarité*, or
call her to order for disrespect to the solem-
nity of justice. His human sympathies and
his sense of humour prevailed.

' Ma sœur,' he said, and his sharp eyes
twinkled unjudiciously as they peered at her
through his glasses, ' your doctrine concern-
ing faith and testimony differs *in toto* from
that of the court. There are witnesses to
prove that on the 10th inst. the prisoner was
present at the meeting in question, and that
evidence makes fatally against her, unless
you can bring forward witnesses to swear
that she was in some other place that day
while the meeting was going on.'

Marguerite's face lighted up with a triumph-
ant expression.

'On the 10th?' she said.   'At what hour
was the meeting, M. le Président?'

'From one in the afternoon to past three.'

'Then I can swear, and bring others to
swear, that she was not present at it!   She
was with me, visiting a sick child.'

There was a sudden excitement in the
court at this.

'You are sure of that, ma sœur?'

'I am perfectly sure of it.'

'And you say there were others present?'

Marguerite hesitated a moment: Antoine
Drex and his old mother were not imposing
witnesses to bring forward.

'There was a crowd outside who saw us
both come out of the house where Mademoiselle Larik had been singing to the child.
I can easily find out some of the people who
were there.'

Marguerite was conscious of a certain
collapse in the strength of her testimony
when it came to producing it; but the court
was with her, and she felt it.   Her own
word, her oath, would weigh with them and

with the jury more than a score of the most creditable witnesses that could be brought forward, and the timid humility which seemed to make her forget this, and lose sight of her own value altogether, only made her more admirable and sympathetic. A rare and winning advocate she was in her weakness and her courage, her pathos and her humour, clothed in the garb of that voluntary poverty which, in its heroic renunciations, represents the most persuasive power on earth.

'And you can swear yourself that you were with her on the 10th at the hour named?' said the judge.

'I can swear it. She came down to the House just after our dinner, and she stayed with me till I went out, and then came with me to Antoine Drex's room, where she sang a little sick child to sleep.'

There was a murmur of sympathy from every part of the court; it rose almost to a cheer. Narka's eyes were fixed on Marguerite as if she could not look away; the half-fierceness had melted out of her face, and, in spite of her immobility, those dark eyes, burning under her level brows, betrayed the relenting emotion that was invading and disarming her.

The judge was going to speak, when a movement at the door arrested his attention. A messenger full of haste pushed his way to the judgment-seat, and a short parley followed between him and the judge.

Marguerite had recognised the Commissary of Police from La Villette. She was alarmed, but not much surprised, when, on turning from the judge, he came straight up to her. The curiosity of the audience was greatly excited, and it was not allayed when the Commissary, having made some communication to Marguerite, which she received with evident horror and amazement, hurried away with her from the court.

It had seemed to Narka before entering the court that no chance of escape, or acquittal, remained to her, and in crossing the threshold of the judgment-hall she had left all hope outside; but as the trial went on, and nothing transpired to incriminate Basil, and as one witness after another failed to substantiate any charge against herself, her spirits rose : she began to hope, and she began to tremble. The only serious point made against her was by Olga Borzidoff, who had sworn to her presence at the meeting on the 10th, and to her having been designated there to give the signal for throwing the bomb-shell ; but this false testimony had been wholly refuted by Marguerite, who had carried the court along with her, and turned the current of justice and of public sentiment strongly in favour of the prisoner.

The judge himself shared this general feeling, but there was nothing in his countenance or manner which had led Narka to suspect it; and when, using his judicial prerogative of addressing and questioning the prisoner as often and as freely as he thought fit, he suddenly began to interrogote her again, she felt herself at a grievous disadvantage. The stony phlegm of despair had deserted her, the revival of hope made her heart beat;

she was nervous and excited; and there was a perceptible tremor in her voice, very unlike the clear metallic tones of some hours ago.

'Can you recall any circumstance,' demanded the judge, 'which would help to prove the alibi sworn to by the last witness?'

'I can, M. le Président,' Narka answered quickly; 'I had lost my voice for more than a month, and that day, when I was with Sœur Marguerite, it suddenly returned. It was very unexpected, and I was greatly excited by it; so was Sœur Marguerite.'

'Can you call any witness to prove that you had lost your voice before that day?'

'Yes; M. le Docteur X—— could certify to the fact; he gave me a consultation not long before. I do not recall the date; but he probably could.'

The judge was going to put another question, when a note was passed up to him. He read it, and recognised the signature as that of a detective well known to the authorities, and highly esteemed for his honesty and skill.

'You may sit down,' the judge said to Narka. Then he added, 'Let Jean Godart come forward.'

A middle-aged man, dressed like a well-to-do workman, stepped into the witness-box.

Narka's heart began to sink again with terror. Was this a false witness come to spring a mine under her feet ?

The witness having stated his name and surname, and his trade of cabinet-maker, the judge said :

'You were present that afternoon when the prisoner sang in the room occupied by Antoine Drex and his mother ?'

'M. le Président, I was amongst the crowd under the window, and I waited to see the singer come out. I wanted badly to see her. I did not see her face well, for she wore a veil, and a hat that came down over her forehead ; but I noticed her figure.'

'Was the prisoner alone ?'

'No; she was with Sœur Marguerite. It
was Sœur Marguerite who told us she had
been singing to the sick child.'

'Why did you want so badly to see the
prisoner?'

'Because of her voice: it was the most
wonderful voice I ever heard. I am fond of
a good song. It is my *petit vice.* I spend
many a franc on a ticket up with the gods
when a great singer comes to Paris. I have
heard the best of them these twenty years
past, but I never heard anything like the
voice of the person who sang that day in the
Cour des Chats.'

'What was it like? Describe it to the
court.'

The witness shook his head.

'It would be a difficult thing to describe,'
he said, with a humorous smile; 'but if these
gentlemen'—looking up at the jury—'can
fancy a score of nightingales in a woman's
throat, with old cognac and oil poured out
all together, they will have some idea of the
effect.'

The jury were evidently amused, and the public laughed.

'You would know the voice if you heard it again ?'

'Parbleu! If I would know it! It made the blood run warm in my veins. I should know it amongst a thousand !'

'You remember what the song was ?'

'The first was——'

'Stop!' interrupted the judge quickly; 'write down the name, and send it up to me.'

While the witness proceeded to do as he was desired, a movement rose and spread in the court. It was arrested immediately when the judge, after reading the paper handed up from the witness, said to the prisoner:

'Can you tell the court what you sang that day ?'

'I sang first a Russian ballad, and then "Mignon's Lament." '

Narka's countenance, for all her self-control, showed plainly with what intense anxiety she was waiting to hear whether the testimony of the detective would corroborate this answer. The court, too, was hushed in breathless expectation.

'The witness,' said the judge, 'has written, " A song in a language I did not understand, and then a song in French that ended, at every verse, *Laissez-moi mourir !"'*

A perfect shout of exultation rose from every part of the hall. Narka flushed crimson, and then grew very white ; she had to clutch the rail in front of her, to save herself from falling.

The prisoner's counsel now followed with his plea, and then the jury retired to consider the verdict.

They returned in ten minutes with one of acquittal.

CHAPTER XX.

LARCHOFF'S MURDERER.

IVAN GORFF had deemed it more prudent, both for Narka and for himself, not to be present at the trial, where there was sure to be a large contingent of Russian spies, as well as French detectives. But when the day of the trial came he found it hard to keep away. The suspense and anxiety were almost unbearable. It was not possible to stay quietly indoors, so he went out and walked about the streets like a troubled spirit, going from one haunt to another, as if something unexpected might turn up to help Narka, or throw light on the unknown authors of her arrest. The more he

thought of it, the stronger grew his fear that
Schenk had betrayed her. The idea, which
had at first been repulsed as a groundless
suspicion, took shape when he found that
Schenk had left town the day before the
arrest; and then, as the days went by, and
he neither came nor wrote, suspicion grew,
and hardened into conviction. Ivan had
quickly detected the German's passion for
Narka, and shrewdly suspected that Schenk
had declared it ; and if so, he had of course
been scornfully rejected. As Ivan paced the
streets he pictured to himself the scene :
Narka startled into indignant surprise, answering him with two flashes of lightning
from her dark eyes, and Schenk, goaded out
of his cold-blooded sleekness, pressing his
suit ; then perhaps threatening—for she was
in his power to an extent. Ivan's blue eyes
scintillated with inextinguishable laughter as
he clenched his hands, swinging heavily by
his side, and tramped on.

Partly drawn by these cogitations, and
partly obeying the blind impulse that

prompted him to pursue his aimless march, he walked on to La Villette and to Narka's house. The place looked just as if nothing had happened; she might have been sitting inside at her work; the door on the street stood open as usual. Ivan stepped in. It was dark in the narrow entry after the brilliant sunshine, but there was light enough for him to see a man standing at the door of the landlady's rooms, opposite to Narka's, as if waiting to be let in. Ivan at a glance recognised Schenk.

The two were equally surprised to meet.

'Oh, it is you!' said Schenk, coming forward, and he held out his hand.

Ivan fell back a step.

'How much money did they give you for it?' he said, hissing out the words between his teeth.

'What do you mean?' demanded Schenk.

'You know what I mean. How much did they give you for selling Narka Larik to the police here?'

'Look here,' said Schenk, and he came

a step nearer, fixing his green eyes on Ivan's, that were blazing like a tigers; 'take back that lie, or I'll knock it down your throat!'

Ivan clenched his hand, and hit out at him; but Schenk, stepping aside in time, avoided the blow, and Ivan struck the wall with his might, breaking his knuckles with the violence of the collision. The pain blinded and maddened him for a moment, and before he had recovered his senses, Schenk drew his cane-sword and ran him through the body. Ivan staggered, and then fell heavily to the ground.

Schenk knelt down, wiped his blade carefully in his victim's coat, slipped it back into the cane, and walked away.

Nobody passed through the entry for nearly an hour. Then a lace-mender who lived on the fifth story came down, and, hurrying out, knocked her foot against the prostrate body. Her scream brought in a woman who was passing.

'A man murdered!' exclaimed the two,

peering down at the white face, and then at the pool of blood around.

In five minutes a crowd had collected ; in five more the Commissary of Police was there, taking down the *procès-verbal*. Before he had finished the doctor arrived.

' Life is not extinct,' said the medical man, after putting his ear to Ivan's heart. ' Is there a room where he could be taken, close by, here on the ground-floor ?'

Some one ran to the concierge and got the key of Narka's door, and Ivan was lifted in and laid upon the bed. Then restoratives were quickly applied, and the wound was attended to. Gradually consciousness returned.

Ivan carried his blank gaze round the room, and began to realize where he was.

' Have they condemned her ?' he asked, in a faint voice.

' Ah! it was, then, a woman ?' said the Commissary, and out came his pencil to add this point to the *procès-verbal*. ' Do you know her ? Could you identify her ?' Then, as Ivan only stared at him vacantly, ' The woman who stabbed you ?' he explained. ' Try and remember. We found you lying in the entry badly wounded. Do you know who stabbed you ?'

But the wounded man turned his head away, and moaned impatiently. At a sign from the doctor the Commissary collapsed.

' He is too weak ; he has lost a deal of blood. I must go down to the Sisters and get some one to come up and attend to him,' said the medical man.

' Sœur Marguerite,' Ivan said, with an effort ; ' tell Sœur Marguerite to come to me.'

Everybody at La Villette knew that Sœur Marguerite was away at the trial.

' I will ask for Sœur Marguerite,' replied the doctor ; ' but she may not be in the way ; I must take whoever is.'

' No, no ; Sœur Marguerite,' Ivan insisted ; ' if she is still in the court, send and say I want to see her ; I have something to say, and there is no time to lose. Be quick !'

The Commissary, guessing that the something was connected with this attempt on
his life, hurried out and called a cab, and
drove to the court, where, as we know, he
found Marguerite, and took her back with
him.

The errand had been done with great
haste, but Ivan's feverish impatience had
found the time never-ending.

'Ah! you are come; thank God!' he exclaimed the moment she appeared. 'Get a
pencil, and write what I am going to tell you.'

' But you are too weak; I had better wait,'
she urged gently.

' No, no; there is no time. I have
strength enough, if only there be time.
Write.'

Marguerite drew her big pocket-book from
her sleeve, and held her pencil ready.

' You remember that All Souls Eve at
Yrakow?' Ivan began. ' My sister Sophie
was coming through the wood in the afternoon. She met Larchoff. He stopped her,
and——' A spasm passed over Ivan's face;

he struggled for a moment with pain, or with emotion, and having mastered it, went on : 'She escaped from him. . . . I saw her flying across the road towards our gate ; she was half mad. . . . I went straight into the sacristy, and took Father Christopher's gun. . . . I knew where he kept it, and I knew it was loaded. . . . I hurried back to the forest, and overtook Larchoff, and shot him.'

Marguerite uttered a cry, and dropped the pencil ; she picked it up, and Ivan continued :

'As God hears me, my first thought was for Sophie ! . . . I wanted to screen her ; if it was known I had killed Larchoff, it would have led to suspicion. . . . After I fired the shot, Father Christopher passed ; he was hurrying through the wood to get back to the confessional ; I thought he might have seen me, and if he had, I knew he would suspect me. I went on to the sacristy, and put back the gun where I had found it. And then—oh, my God, how shall I tell it !—then I went into the chapel, and knelt down in the confessional and confessed the murder. After

that I was safe.   I knew that this sealed his
lips : that he must let himself be put to death
rather than utter a word that might incriminate
me, and betray the secret of the confessional.
. . . The next day I went into X——, and
denounced him as the murderer.'

Marguerite could bear no more ; she
burst into tears, overcome with horror and
compassion.

'Ah! I have suffered for my crime!' Ivan
went on ; 'ay, the torments of the damned.
. . . It so chanced—God in His judgment
so decreed—that I was passing when the
police were carrying him away. . . . I saw
him driven on between the two policemen.
Oh, my God ! my God ! the look he gave me !
. . . it has haunted me like the curse in a dead
man's eye. . . . I felt sure at first that the Prince
would have obtained his release ; when that
failed, I did what I could. . . . I spent my
whole fortune trying to purchase his escape,
bribing the gaolers, trying to get alleviations
for him.   I have lived in poverty . . . my life
has been a hell of remorse. . . . And now I

am dying accursed and unforgiven, murdered
myself. . . . It is just! it is just!'

Marguerite dropped on her knees, shaken
to her soul with pity for the miserable man
who had sinned and suffered so terribly.
But her strong sense and habit of self-restraint
quickly brought her back to the practical question of how to make this confession available
for Father Christopher. She had presence
of mind enough to remember that either it
must be made verbally before another witness,
or Ivan must sign what she had written in
presence of a witness.

'Is it any good my confessing now?' said
Ivan, as if he guessed what was in her
mind. 'Will it help to set Father Christopher free, do you think? If it did, if I
knew that before I died, it would make hell
less horrible to me.'

'I have not a doubt,' replied Marguerite,
'but that as soon as your statement is known
to the authorities, they will liberate him at
once; but you will have to repeat the confession, or else sign it in the presence of

another person. May I send for the Commissary?'

'Yes, yes; send for as many as will come. I will swear before the whole world that I committed the murder, and confessed it to Father Christopher.'

Marguerite went out, intending to send for the Commissary. She found him in the entry, surrounded by the curé, the doctor, several police-officers, and others who had been attracted by the news of the murder. She told rapidly what had happened, and when the Commissary, accompanied by the curé and the doctor, came in, she read aloud what she had written, and then asked Ivan if it was correct, and if he would swear to the truth of the story.

'Yes, I swear, as a dying man, that what you have written is true. So help me God! Get me up that I may sign it.'

They lifted him, and put the pen in his hand, and he wrote his name; the others then added their signatures. The Commissary was putting away the pen, when

Ivan made a sign that he wanted it again.
They gave it to him, and he fingered it
fondly : it was Narka's pen. He remembered seeing it on her little writing-
table.

'What have they done to her?' he
asked—'to Narka Larik ; what is the
sentence ?'

'She is acquitted on all points,' replied
the Commissary, who had heard the news
from a police-officer just come from the
court.

'Thank God !' muttered Ivan, and his face
brightened ; then, changing suddenly, a look
of hungry, wolfish hate came over it. 'Now
let them catch Schenk !' he said ; 'it was
Schenk's doing ; it was Schenk that stabbed
me. I would die easy if I knew they would
hang him !'

He fell back exhausted on the pillow.

CHAPTER XXI.

THE verdict of acquittal was re-
ceived with loud and long
applause, the Villette element
making itself conspicuous in the chorus by
yells of triumph, which might have easily
been mistaken for howls of rage.

When M. de Beaucrillon and Sibyl led
Narka out of the court, half fainting, she
hardly knew where she was going, and
allowed herself to be assisted into the carriage without asking where they were taking
her. It was only when she found herself
before the steps of Sibyl's house that she
realized where she was. It was then too

late to protest, even if she had had strength to do it.

Sibyl led her upstairs, and put her to bed; she was kind and tender as a sister; and Narka, worn out in mind and body, submitted unresistingly to her soft ministrations. She was thankful to be at rest. She slept through the night from sheer exhaustion. Sibyl would have her lie in bed next morning; she forbade her to get up till the afternoon, and gave orders that Mademoiselle Narka was not to be disturbed, even if Sœur Marguerite came.

Immediately after the second breakfast, Sibyl went out with Gaston. They were both anxious to see Marguerite, and learn the cause of her mysterious summons from court the day before.

The moment they were gone, Narka rose, and dressed herself, and slipped down to the boudoir. She could not lie quiet in bed, when Basil might arrive at any moment and call for her. She had not been long in the boudoir when a carriage drove into the court.

It might be Basil! Narka started up and went to the window. A coupé was drawn up before the steps, and the hall-porter was parleying with some one inside. Presently he opened the carriage-door and assisted a lady to alight. Narka recognised Marie Krinsky. A meeting with this girl, who loved Basil, who had been her rival, would have been intolerable ; but it did not occur to her that Marie was coming upstairs : she was, no doubt, going to wait in the drawing-room, or perhaps to write a note in the library. It was only when the sound of silk rustling on the landing became audible that Narka knew the young Princess was about to appear. She glanced round for a way of escape. There was a panelled door that opened into a tiny closet, a sort of *débarras* where the tea-table, etc., were kept. There was just time to spring across the room and open this door and draw it after her, without daring to shut it, when Marie entered.

'You will find everything here, Princess,' said the servant, and soon the click of an opened inkstand, and then the noise of a pen scratching the paper, announced that Marie was writing.

The time seemed long to Narka, but in reality ten minutes had not elapsed when Marie started up, exclaiming:

'Sœur Marguerite! I am so glad! I was writing a line for Madame de Beaucrillon. We only returned from Fontainebleau last night. You were at the trial; tell me about it. Is Narka Larik guilty? Did she really conspire against the life of the Emperor?'

Marguerite lifted her eyebrows.

'Why, did you not read the trial? It is all in this morning's newspapers. She was completely acquitted.'

'Oh, I know that. M. de Beaucrillon is rich enough to buy up the jury. And he was quite right to do it; but is she guilty? Is she the dreadful woman they say? I so want to know the truth!'

She spoke earnestly, nervously.

'Narka is no more guilty than I am,' said Marguerite, with the warmth of conviction;

' she is a noble woman, and she has suffered cruelly.'

' Ah! But now they say—— Is it true, this story of Prince Basil's being in love with her, and wanting to marry her ?'

' Yes, it is quite true.'

Marie grew pale, and Marguerite saw that the words had cut into her like a knife. Poor child! So she was to be a victim, through no fault of her own. She looked as if a touch would have overthrown her courage; but she struggled bravely, and kept up.

' I am glad she is good, since he is going to marry her,' she said ; ' it would have been dreadful for Madame de Beaucrillon ; and I should have been very sorry for her brother, who——'

Marie stopped short, blushed violently, and then grew white, and an expression between terror and defiance came into her eyes. Marguerite turned to see what had wrought the sudden change, and saw a gentleman advancing quickly towards the open door of the

boudoir ; he was unkempt and travel-stained,
like one come off a journey ; but Marguerite
recognised Basil at a glance.   He went
straight up to her, and took her hand and
raised it to his lips ; he did not say a
word, but his face, his whole manner, were
eloquent with feeling.   Suddenly, as if he
had not noticed the presence of the young
Princess, he made her a low bow.

Marie took up her parasol.

' I am not sending you away, I hope,
Princess,' said Basil.

' No ; I was going.'

She shook hands with Marguerite, and
then, looking Basil steadily in the face :

' I am glad to be one of the first to congratulate you on your approaching marriage,
Prince,' she said.

He read insolent contempt in her glance ;
but it was only the defiance of desperation.

' Thank you, Princess,' he replied, and
held back the portière with an ostentatious
pretence of making wider room for her
exit.

The girl's retreating footsteps made no
sound on the soft carpet, and Narka did
not know she had left the room when Basil
spoke :

'Sibyl is out ?'

'Yes ; I believe she is gone to La Villette,'
Marguerite replied, and she laid on the table
a parcel that she took out of a basket on her
arm.

There was nothing so far to inform Narka
that Marie was not still present.

Marguerite looked tired, and Basil thought
agitated ; she sat down, and, with a certain
hesitation in her manner :

'A dreadful thing has happened,' she said ;
'Ivan Gorff was stabbed yesterday during the
trial.'

'Good God ! Ivan ! By whom ?'

'By a man named Schenk.'

'Schenk !' Basil repeated, aghast. 'My
God ! And is Ivan dead !'

'He is dying. He sent for me to make
a confession—a terrible confession.' Narka
held her breath, while Marguerite paused,

as if the words were hard to speak. Then, almost in a whisper : ' *It was Ivan who murdered Larchoff!*'

Basil's vehement exclamation covered another sound that came at the same moment from the wall behind him. He dropped into a chair, too stunned to utter a word.

Narka felt sure they were alone now ; but she also was too stunned to speak or move ; her heart gave a great leap, and then sank ; she felt sick and faint, but she remained motionless, rooted to the ground.

' Marguerite,' Basil said, ' if you knew what this revelation is to me !'

' I do know,' she answered, in a low voice, and her lids fell.

Basil stood up.

' You suspected me of the murder ?'

' I thought you had done it accidentally.'

' And you kept my secret ! Marguerite !— Marguerite !'

Before she could start up, or prevent him, he had fallen down before her, and was sobbing with his head upon her knees. Marguerite was too frightened by the suddenness of the action and by the violence of his emotion to know what to do; Basil, however, mastered the paroxysm quickly, and stood up, and sat down beside her.

Narka had by this time regained her self-possession; but she had no longer the courage to come out of her hiding-place. She had first listened involuntarily to the dialogue, and now she could not show herself; it was too late. She heard Basil sobbing, and she guessed, more by instinct than by sound, that he had fallen down at Marguerite's feet; if her life had depended on it, she could not have pushed open the door and looked at him there.

'Yes,' he went on, after a moment's silence, 'I thought I had shot him; but I was not certain. When Father Christopher was arrested, I knew it was too late to accuse myself; the police had fastened the crime on him. The only thing I could do was to go to St. Petersburg and sue for his release. I came away, believing he was to be set free the next

day. Did Ivan tell you why he murdered
Larchoff?'

'Yes; he confessed everything. It was a
terrible story.' And she repeated it as Ivan
had told it.

'My God! how horrible!'

Basil rose and walked the length of the
room; then he sat down near Marguerite
again, and, speaking deliberately, like a man
who was constrained to give utterance to
something that would not be held back:

'I, too, have a confession to make,' he said:
'that murder changed my whole destiny—
perhaps. I had set my heart on making you
my wife. There was an end of that hope the
moment I felt there was blood upon my
hands; but I loved you as I have never
loved any other woman.'

Both were too absorbed to notice the dull
sound of something falling heavily to the
ground close by.

'Oh, Basil! and Narka?' Marguerite said, in
a tone of pained reproach. 'You love Narka?'

'Yes, I love Narka, and I will do my best

to make her happy. I will be a good husband to her; she shall miss nothing; but
my love for you was a unique thing in
my life.'

The moment was too solemn, Basil himself was too free from self-consciousness, for
the strange avowal to make Marguerite feel
shy, to cause her any embarrassment. It
was a startling confession for her to listen
to; but it told her nothing she had not
known before. She knew perfectly well
that night at Yrakow that the course of her
destiny was suddenly changed. It was all
like a dream. She looked back to the dream
now, and saw spread out before her, like a
landscape seen in a looking-glass, the life
that might have been : a panorama of golden
days crowned with honours and delights; but
the vision stirred no shadow of regret in her
heart, nor did it move her will to a momentary
recoil from the part that she had chosen. Far
from it : she rejoiced that her present lot
was beyond the reach of change. With an
almost involuntary movement she felt for

her crucifix, and closed her hand upon it, silently renewing her self-consecration.

Basil, too, had been carried back to the past, but not with the same glad assent in its renunciations.

'My God!' he cried, with a sudden burst of passionate feeling, 'it is as if a reprieve had suddenly come to me, after being under sentence of condemnation all these years!'

'Thank God!' Marguerite exclaimed fervently. 'And now you will give up once and for ever these wild and wicked theories that have led you and Narka into such trouble? God has been very good to you, and you owe Him a return. You have now an opportunity of redeeming the past; you must begin from this forth a noble and useful life; you must break off with conspiracy and revolution, and work for your country in wiser and better ways. Promise me that you will.'

Basil fell back and thrust his hands into his pockets.

'If I had only myself to think of,' he said,

after a pause ; ' but I have contracted en-
gagements that it would not be honourable
to break ; it would be cowardly to abandon
those who are risking, and who will go on to
the bitter end risking, their lives for the sake
of overthrowing tyrants.'

' That is just nonsense, rank nonsense !'
protested Marguerite, with her old impulsive
manner. ' They will never overthrow anybody but themselves. I know them well : a
set of hot-headed fools and fanatics ! I see
them every day, and I hear the wild nonsense
they talk. But what is excusable as folly in
many of them, is downright criminal in you ;
and your example would give many of them
the courage and the excuse to give up the
whole thing—be sure of that. There are
very few in Russia, I dare say, as in France,
who after a while do not see the madness
of the work they have embarked in, and
who would not gladly get out of it if they
could. Besides, you are not worth much to
them ; you will never go far enough to do
the work they want ; you think that talking

and writing and stirring up passionate desires
for liberty is doing a grand thing ; but they
want it to lead to action—that is, to assassination, to wholesale murder.   You will never
lend your hand to that ; you will only go far
enough to ruin yourself, without satisfying
them.   Give it up.   Oh, Basil ! for Heaven's
sake give it up, and begin to lead an honourable, useful life.   Narka will make it a happy
life for you.   She will be as noble and loyal
and loving a wife as any man was ever blest
with.   Think, too, of all that she has suffered
for your sake !   All but death.   Yes, that
time in the fortress was worse than death.
Make it up to her now, and guard her, at any
rate in the future, from those horrors that she
has gone through in the past.   She was very
near falling into the hands of the torturers
again.   It is almost a miracle that she has
escaped.   A man whom we had helped in
trouble waylaid the policeman and rescued
this,' Marguerite continued, taking the casket
from the table.

    ' Do you know what is in it ?' Basil asked,

as he took it in his hand, and tore off the
paper that covered it.

'The papers you gave her to keep, and
those revolutionary articles of yours that
Ivan Gorff gave her to translate.'

'Good heavens!' Basil exclaimed, greatly
excited. The sight of that ivory box brought
back his boyhood to him; he remembered
the morning he gave it to Narka full of
sweetmeats for her birthday; he kept turning it round and examining it to conceal
his emotion. 'My poor Narka!' he murmured.

'You will make it all up to her now; promise me you will?' Marguerite pleaded.
'You will give up conspiracy?'

Basil did not answer. He was moved to
his centre; but his will was torn in opposite
directions: pity and tenderness for Narka
drew him one way; what he called honour
drew him another.

'Basil,' Marguerite said, and the blood
mounted to her cheek, and her voice
trembled, 'you say that you cared for me

once; for the sake of that old affection, to prove to me that it was something deeper and better than a passing fancy, promise me what I ask you. I ask it in the name of God, of your mother, of all that you ever held sacred !'

Her voice broke a little, and her eyes were full of tears.

Still Basil hesitated; but it was only because he was struggling with the emotion that choked him.

'I promise you,' he answered.

There was a pause, and then Marguerite said :

'Now all our prayers must be that the reprieve may reach Father Christopher in time.'

She stayed on a few minutes, asking questions about the distance to Irkoutsk, calculating the chances and perils that must be reckoned with on the way homeward. Then she rose to go.

'You won't wait to see Narka ?' Basil said.

'No; she is perhaps asleep, or at any rate she is resting. You will tell her about Ivan; his confession will be an immense relief to her; but the rest will be a great shock. She will be horrified, too, to hear about Schenk.'

Basil accompanied Marguerite downstairs. In the hall he said:

'I wonder would they let me see Ivan? Could you get me into the prison? I should like to see him once.'

'Oh! yes, do go and see him; I am sure it will be a consolation to the poor fellow. Go to-morrow morning at nine o'clock, and ask for Sœur Jeanne; or, stay, if you go there now, you will find her. Say that you have a message to her from Sœur Marguerite, and the porter will let you in.'

'I will go at once,' said Basil; 'and by the time I get back, Narka will probably be up, and able to see me.'

He stood and watched Marguerite till she crossed the court and disappeared. Then he went out and called a cab, and drove to the prison.

As Marguerite walked rapidly homeward, she felt nearer to perfect happiness than she had ever done before in her innocent, happy life. The windows of the world seemed to have been suddenly thrown wide open, and fresh air from heaven let in to blow about her face. Her heart was so merry that she could have sung for gladness. All the wrong things were coming right. If only La Villette would cast out its heart of rage! Marguerite kept her hand upon that angry heart as a sicknurse feels the pulse of a patient; *le pauvre peuple* was her sick child; she kept feeling its pulse, and the quick, irregular beats made her anxious.

'If only I might die for them,' she murmured in her heart, with a sinking of despair. But then she thought of Father Christopher, and of Basil and Narka, and how all the wrong things were coming right at last, and she trusted and rejoiced.

CHAPTER XXII.

RENUNCIATION.

ARKA lay motionless, crouching in a heap on the ground, for some minutes after Basil and Marguerite had left the room. At last the silence assured her that they had gone. She rose to her knees, and dragged herself up, and opened the door cautiously; there were the two chairs that Marguerite and Basil had been sitting on; they seemed to hold them still. The atmosphere of the place was suffocating; Narka felt she must get out of it to breathe; she made her way up to her own room, and sat down and tried to think what had happened since she had left it, only an hour ago.

The whole world was changed to her, and yet in reality those words of Basil's which had flung her down as if stricken with paralysis had told her nothing new ; she was conscious of having known all along that in those early days at Yrakow he had loved Marguerite, and on the night of the murder Marguerite had betrayed the secret of her love for him.   But then had come the warrant and the ransom, and his declaration to herself ; and what waves of passionate love and trust had swept over their lives since then, obliterating the very trace of those early jealousies and uncertainties !

Narka was not so simple as to suppose that a man's love was not to be trusted, because the virgin vintage of his heart had been thrown into the wine-press for another woman's feet to tread.   She would not have felt a pang of jealousy or resentment if Basil had himself confessed to her that he had loved Marguerite first ; but that he should never have said a word to her, and should now confess it to Marguerite—this stung her to the quick, and struck at the root of all belief in his love.

'If he loved me,' she repeated to herself, 'he would have been compelled by the very force of his love to tell me ; he could not have kept it from me.'

And she was right. For though we may sometimes wholly trust where we do not love, we can never wholly love where we do not trust. Basil, then, did not love her ; not as she understood love ; not as a man should love the woman he is going to marry. And if he did not love her, should she keep him to his engagement ? Could she let him sacrifice himself to her from a sense of honour, of pity, of gratitude ?

Schenk was right ; Basil had never loved her.

Narka interlaced her fingers, and straightened up her arms above her head in a gesture of intolerable anguish.

'I will give him up !—I will give him up !' she cried aloud, almost in a shout, and then she flung herself upon the sofa, and sobbed

till it shook under her.   When the paroxysm
had subsided, she stood up, and began to
walk up and down the room.   'If he were to
confess the truth to me even now, I would
believe him,' she said, again speaking aloud
to herself, and like a drowning man catching
at a straw in her despair ; 'if he were to
come to me now and say : " I loved Marguerite in the old days before I learned to
love you," I could believe——'

But she suddenly checked herself.   Had
he not told Marguerite that his love for
her was a unique thing in his life ?   And
then he had said that Narka should miss
nothing, that he would be a loyal and
loving husband to her, that he would pay
back his debt as a man of honour.   O God !
was this the return she was to get for
her passionate love !   Could she take such
pitiful payment of cold gratitude and duty in
exchange for the love that had been burning
like a fire in her heart all these years ?   No ;
it was intolerable.   'I will give him up !' she
repeated, already with a stern quietness that

bespoke a firmer will than her first violent outburst.

She sat down and tried to face the reality. She would give him up; this much was certain; she was resolved to give him up. And having made this tremendous decision, it seemed as if the necessity for it grew suddenly clearer. She saw distinctly, like something new that she had never even glanced at before, what the consequences would be to Basil and to herself if he married her: he was going to make as complete a sacrifice as a man could make for a woman; he was going to quarrel with his father; to give him up; to give up his whole fortune and position; to give up Sibyl too, for though she might feign to forgive the marriage, in her heart she would never really forgive it, and she would hate the woman who had come between her and the brother of whom she was so proud. And what had Narka to offer him in return for all this? If he had loved her! . . . ah, if he had loved her! Narka knew with what supreme abundance love can satisfy the lover, and make all sacrifices as nothing compared to the plenary bliss it can bestow. But he did not love her.

'I will not marry him; I will not see him again,' she said; and as her will took firmer hold of this determination, it seemed to harden her heart and brace it for the sacrifice. Then, instinctively, her thoughts flew to Marguerite. There would be sympathy there and under-standing. 'I will tell her the truth; I will tell her everything,' was Narka's reflection. But when she had told Marguerite, what was she to do? Where was she to go? She must take up life again with its difficulties and its inexorable necessities; she must go back to loneliness, without any sustaining hope to make it endurable. Suddenly she remembered Zampa, and the thought was like a flash of lightning showing her a way out of the darkness. She would go to Zampa; she would throw herself into the art she loved, and enter at once on her career as a singer, and study with all her might, and become a great artist. A thrill of relief,

almost of exultation, came with this resolution, and with the consciousness that she
had within her the power to fashion her own
destiny, and conquer independence. She
need not be an object of pity to anyone ;
there was something in this. Narka stood
up again. There was a knock at the door.
One of the maids, of course. She said,
' Come in.'

The door opened, and Basil entered.

He went quickly up to her, and took her
in his arms.

' Narka !' he cried, straining her to him.

She suffered his embrace without re-
sponding to it ; Basil was too excited to
notice this, but he felt that she was
trembling.

' I was here before,' he said, ' but you
were resting. How are you, dearest ? Let
me look at you ? You are tired and pale.
No wonder.' He kissed her forehead. ' Sit
down beside me ;' and he would have
drawn her to the couch, but Narka did not
move.

'Tell me about Ivan,' she said. 'Have you seen him? Is he dead?'

'No; he is still alive; but they don't think he will pass the day.'

Basil now became conscious of something strange about her. It was natural that the horror of this tragedy should have solemnized all things to them both, that it should be uppermost in her thoughts, and have checked the overflow of her joy a little; but there was something beyond this in her manner. He tried again to draw her to the couch, but her figure stiffened against his arm and she laid her hand upon his shoulder, as if gently putting him from her.

'What is the matter, Narka? Are you not glad to see me?' he asked.

'I have something to say to you,' she said, and her great eyes looked steadily into his, and her voice did not falter: 'There is an end of our engagement. You must leave me, and forget that you ever thought of marrying me.'

Basil drew away his arm, and looked at her in amaze.

'You are mad,' he said. Then in a softer
tone : 'No wonder if you were, after all you
have been going through, my poor Narka!
But what has put this folly into your
head ?'

'It is no folly. The folly was when we
thought that our marriage could bring either
of us anything but suffering and regret. Yes
Let me speak out, Basil. Listen to me. If
you married me, you would lose everything ;
you would be an exile all your life ; your
father would never forgive you, nor Sibyl ;
and Sibyl would hate me ; and I could not
live under that—it would kill me. I see it
all now. We must part. You will marry
some one who will suit you and make you
happy ; some one in your own rank. Marie
Krinsky loves you ; marry her, and give up
playing at patriotism ; you are not made for
it. No, dear Basil, you are made to be what
you are, and nothing else. If you broke
with your kindred and your caste, and married me, we should both regret it. You
would try to hide it from me, but I should

see it, and it would make me a miserable woman.'

She said all this rapidly, as if she were in a hurry to get it all out before breaking down ; but her voice did not break, although it was nervous and vibrating, and she was so white that Basil feared she was going to faint ; but her eyes still met his without quailing. What did it all mean ? What had she heard to drive her to this extraordinary resolution ? His conscience smote him ; he remembered his words to Marguerite in the boudoir ; but they could not have come back to Narka.

'Sibyl has been talking to you,' he said ; 'she has persuaded you to this.'

'No, she has not ; I have not had a moment's conversation with Sibyl since I have been in the house. She has had nothing whatever to do with my determination.'

'Then what in Heaven's name has come to you, Narka ? Have you ceased to care for me ? It was only yesterday you swore to me you loved me as your life, and now you coolly turn me away, and throw me off without a word of explanation. I insist upon knowing what it means.'

'I have told you,' she replied. 'We have been living in a fool's paradise. I was blind, and you were mad. But there is an end of it. We must separate. Don't be sorry for me, or afraid. I have courage; I will go on my way safely.'

'Good God! what are you talking about? What way will you go, if you do not come with me?'

'I will go to Florence, and become a singer. My voice is better than ever it was. I am able to face the future without any fear.'

She was still as white as marble. There was something marble-like about her altogether, in the calm stony coldness of her manner to him. It was unnatural in so passionate a creature as Narka.

'You are talking mere nonsense, child,' said Basil; 'and besides, you forget that I have a claim on you that is not to be set aside by any fanciful arguments, or caprice of feeling : I am your debtor for fifty thousand roubles.'

' Not quite. You sent me some of it by poor Ivan ; and Sibyl has paid me the whole amount. It is there,' said Narka, pointing to the drawer of the writing-table ; ' I found it when I came here from the court yesterday.'

' Sibyl had no right to meddle in it,' he said, reddening with anger.

He would rather have remained Narka's debtor than become Sibyl's, and it seemed to weaken his hold on Narka that the debt should have been paid ; though, if she persisted in breaking their engagement, it was better he should be free. Would she persist ? Basil assured himself that she would not ; but there was something about Narka that said to him, ' She will.'

If anything had happened a month ago to break off his engagement honourably to himself, it is doubtful whether he would have felt the blow a very severe one; but coming from Narka's hand, and dealt at him in this cool, sudden way, it wounded him to the quick, and fired his feeling towards her to a flame of passion. He would not give her up! He knew how she loved him, and how she had suffered for him. This act of hers was the result of some heroic fancy, or else she had been stung to it by wounded pride. In spite of her denial, he suspected Sibyl was at the bottom of it; but he would conquer her in spite of her own stubborn pride, in spite of Sibyl, and the whole world. There was no use, however, in arguing with Narka now: opposition would only nerve her to more determined resistance.

'Narka, you are very cruel to play with me in this way,' he said, 'and I shall punish you for it some day. But you are tired and nervous, and you want rest after all you have gone through. I wish you could go to the country for a week. Perhaps if you went down to Beaucrillon for a few days, it would do you good and bring you to your right mind.'

'Perhaps,' she said, looking at him with a smile that went to his heart's core: there was an expression in her eyes that was indefinable.

Basil drew her to him, and held her to his breast, kissing her with passionate tenderness.

'You shan't fly from me,' he murmured between the kisses; 'I would follow you to the end of the world if you did. My love! my wife! my beautiful one!'

Narka let herself sink into his embrace. Now, for the first time, she was tasting the caresses of a lover. Basil felt her trembling, and triumphed in his power over her, and silently rejoiced.

A knock at the door made him start, and release her.

'Monsieur de Beaucrillon desires to know if mademoiselle will come downstairs, or receive him here?' said the servant.

'I will come down presently,' Narka replied. But when the man was gone, she said to Basil: 'I must be alone for a while.

I cannot see anyone. Don't let him come up.'

' I will protect you,' Basil said ; and he kissed her again, and turned away.

As he was in the act of opening the door, a sound like a strangled cry made him look back. An extraordinary change had come over Narka : her face, a moment ago white and cold, was flushed and quivering ; her lips were parted, her eyes, liquid with yearning love, looked straight into his ; as he moved towards her, she held out her arms, and, with a sudden spring, fell upon his breast, and clung to him with an embrace that was almost fierce in its passionate transport.

Basil murmured words of endearment as he pressed her to him ; he kissed her again and again, and when she disengaged herself, and gently pushed him from her, he was satisfied to release her, and went away conscious that his power over her was greater than ever, that she loved him too well, for Sibyl, or pride, or anything on earth to induce her to give him up.

Narka waited till the sound of his footfalls on the stairs had quite ceased, and then she flung herself on her knees, and her tortured heart found relief in a flood of tears, while her soul went up in a prayer for pity and help. But it was not in her nature to indulge long in the luxury of grief, to keep action waiting on emotion. She rose and dried her eyes, and considered what she had to do. The vital crisis had come and gone. She was glad to have seen Basil. That last caress had satisfied an intolerable craving of her heart, and given her courage for what remained to be done. Her remaining fears were now cast out; she felt armed against every attack from within and from without. She would have risen and gone away that moment, but for the fear of meeting Basil, or M. de Beaucrillon. Besides, she must write a farewell note to Sibyl, explaining her flight. This done, she put on her cloak and bonnet, and waited. After a while, the bell clanged, the gates were opened, and Sibyl's open carriage came wheeling into the court. Soon

Narka heard a light step on the stairs ; there was a knock at the door, then a pause, and she heard the step descending.

At the end of about half an hour there was a sound of wheels moving away. Narka looked through the lace curtains, and saw Sibyl and M. de Beaucrillon and Basil all driving off together. Basil had kept his promise of protecting her.

She was free now to go. But instead of hurrying away, she sat down. It was not that her purpose faltered ; on the contrary, she felt stronger, more resolute than ever : but suddenly a strange sensation had come over her, something like what she had experienced in the prison. It was as if she had been lifted out of the world, beyond time, and was looking back on all she had left behind, on the broken destiny she was running away from, as one looks back from a turn in the road at the house one has just left. But the mystery of life seemed suddenly illuminated with an altogether different meaning and purpose from what she had seen, or fancied, in that

other vision ; the dark and cruel things were
now bright with hidden possibilities of bless-
ing and redemption. She saw Marguerite's
ideal emerge in all its beauty amidst the
storm and confusion of the world around it ;
and side by side with this she saw her own
ideal overturned and dishonoured. The things
that she had worshipped had betrayed her ;
the love whose incantation had transfigured
her whole life had melted away like a
shadow, and with it all her illusions had
vanished ; the insane theories, the wild en-
thusiasms, which had inspired and misled her,
had simultaneously evaporated with the great
passion that had fed her belief in them.
Only a little while ago, the defeat of those
hopes and dreams would have reckoned
amongst the bitterest of life's revenges ; but
now she was content to let them go. And
was everything gone ? Was there nothing
saved from the wreck ? Yes : there remained
God and her fellow-creatures ; there was still
all humanity to care for. She would open
her heart to this larger love, and put her

hand to whatsoever service of help came to it. In this supreme moment of her sacrifice Narka was beginning to taste something of the inebriation that comes to those who drink with courage of the cup of pain.

But it was time to be going. She rose quickly, and went downstairs. It seemed only yesterday that she had walked up those crimson steps to be greeted by Sibyl in that boudoir where a few hours ago she had heard the sentence that banished her. There was a servant in the hall ; Narka passed him by, and went out into the garden to a gate that opened into the street ; she knew the trick of the latch, lifted it, let herself out, and then drew the gate behind her.

CHAPTER XXIII.

LA SCALA.

IT is winter again at Yrakow. Sibyl and her husband and Basil are once more assembled in that tapestried room where we first saw them. Father Christopher is there too, aged and broken; his figure, formerly so erect, is bent, and he walks like a man who is still carrying a load and dragging a chain; but this, he explains, is only a bad habit that his old limbs cannot get rid of; he declares he is the happiest of men; and, indeed, the serenity of his countenance and his cheerful flow of spirits confirm the assertion.

Basil is engaged to Marie Krinsky, and

the marriage is soon to be celebrated at the Winter Palace with all the pomp becoming the presence of royalty and the rank of the bride and bridegroom.

Sibyl ought to have been satisfied. And yet the old castle was empty of something that she missed at every turn. She was grateful to Narka for having gone of her own free will, and set Basil free; but her absence made a void that nothing could fill. By tacit consent, the brother and sister never spoke of her; but each knew that she was dearer than ever to the other since they had lost her.

This evening M. de Beaucrillon was reading aloud the newspaper, when he came to a paragraph headed, '*Milan.—Extraordinary Scene at La Scala,*' and having read so far, stopped suddenly.

Sibyl looked up from her embroidery-frame.

' What is it ?' she said.

He hesitated a moment and then, with a movement that seemed to say, ' Why not ?' read on :

' " Last night Mademoiselle Narka Larik made her *début* in *Norma,* and no one who witnessed the performance will ever forget the scene. Her extraordinary beauty would alone have insured her a success, but this, joined to her incomparable voice and transcendent talent, won for her such a triumph as was, perhaps, never seen on any stage. The audience were simply mad with enthusiasm. The King of X—— went himself behind the scenes, and conducted the beautiful artist, who was almost overcome with emotion, to the royal box, where the Queen embraced her, and drawing a costly diamond ring from her own finger, placed it on Mademoiselle Narka's. Cries of *' Evviva la Regina !'* *' Evviva la Narka !'* showed how the spectators rejoiced in this meeting of the two royalties of genius and rank. The prima donna is invited to a dinner given in her honour by their Majesties on the twentieth instant." '

A moment of intense silence followed the reading of this passage. Then M. de

Beaucrillon laid down the newspaper, and said :

'She is a noble woman. I hope some Crown Prince will fall in love with her, and marry her !'

THE END.

BILLING AND SONS, PRINTERS, GUILDFORD
G., C. & Co.